The Last White Christmas

The Last White Christmas

A Story by Ronald W. Monchak

Avonstoke Press
Troy, Michigan

This story is fictional. The characters and locales are figments
of the author's imagination. Any similarity to real people or
places is coincidental.

Cover & Illustrations by Timothy Bodendistel
Book Design by Guy Foxxe

Manufactured in the United States of America

1997 1996 1995 1994   5 4 3 2 1

Avonstoke Press
an imprint of
Momentum Books, Ltd.
6964 Crooks Road
Troy, Michigan 48098
U.S.A.

ISBN 1-879094-17-7

Library of Congress Cataloging-in-Publication Data

Monchak, Ronald W., 1935-
    The last white Christmas : a story / by Ronald W. Monchak.
       p.   cm.
     ISBN 1-879094-17-7 :
   PS3563.05167L37   1994
   813'.54--dc20   94-12611

"At this magical time of year,
wishes really can come true."

1

Not a sign of the snow they were praying for. Not even a flake. Chet and Maureen Alcot knew they had made the right decision. They would move themselves and their three kids north even if they had to do it Thanksgiving week.

"It's not going to be much of a Thanksgiving anyway," Chet said as he opened his pay envelope.

He looked to see if his pay was all there. It was. Two weeks plus eight weeks severance. Not a dime more. Not that he was expecting more. After all, he kept telling himself, there is no Santa Claus. That and the problems they were facing gave them very little to be thankful for.

"How much is in your envelope?" he asked Maureen.

"The usual," she said. "I wasn't laid off, remember? I quit."

"Don't rub it in."

"I wasn't rubbing it in," she said quietly.

She was trying to remain sympathetic even

1

though in her heart she was resentful at having to give up the best job she had ever had. But she was still able to put a good face on it. There was nothing else for her to do.

"We agreed this was the right thing to do," Chet said grudgingly. He was trying to put a good face on it too but wasn't doing as good a job. "I was getting tired of driving to Ann Arbor anyway."

Maureen moved to the window and stared at the bare maple in the front yard. There was a glint of tears in her eyes. Chet went up to her and put his arm around her waist.

"Sorry, hon," he said. "I know how much that job meant to you."

"I'll be all right," she said. "Maybe I'll find something like it in Mittenville."

"Like a senior designer in an art studio?" he laughed. "Forget it. You'll be lucky if they know what design is."

"Can't we pretend?" Maureen said grimly. "Isn't this supposed to be the season for pretending?"

Chet felt helpless. He wanted to be able to say something wise and compassionate, something that would make the hurt go away, but he didn't know how. It wasn't his nature.

Maureen wiped the tears away herself and mustered a smile.

"And where do you think you're going to find a publishing company up there?" she asked. "You'll be lucky if they know what a book is."

Chet laughed.

"I'll start my own publishing company," he said and squeezed her again. "I'm sorry, hon. I really am."

"It's not your fault," Maureen said.

"It's not anybody's fault. It's the luck of the draw. We've got to play the cards we're dealt."

"They were dealt to me, not you," Maureen said. "Judy was *my* sister."

"That means they were dealt to me too," Chet said.

She looked at him and kissed him on the cheek. She remembered why she had fallen in love with him in the first place, and it wasn't his good looks.

2

They had sold their small ranch house for a little more than what they owed on it. Now they packed their furniture into a rental truck and loaded their belongings in a used van Chet bought in place of the Bimmer he had just sold.

"Sure is noisy," Maureen said with a nod at the van. "It's attracting attention for blocks."

"Noisy?" Chet was puzzled. "The engine's not even running."

"I mean the decorating."

The decorating, as Maureen called it, was definitely noisy. The van had been owned by a drug dealer and was confiscated in the same raid that had sent him away for twenty years. Chet was able to buy it at the police auction and planned on having it painted as soon as they could afford it. Or if he had to, he'd paint it himself with a spray can.

Chet and Maureen stood in the driveway on that unseasonably warm Thanksgiving Day and took a last look at their once-upon-a-time dream house. It was small, and the bare trees and shrubs made it seem sad. But it was their first home and they loved it. Maureen had fallen in love with it the first day she had found it five years ago. Chet had learned to love it when he remodeled the kitchen. They knew someday they would have to sell it when they traded up for a bigger house. They just never dreamed they would have to give it up so soon.

Their hands touched and their fingers inter-twined.

"This house was always good to us," Maureen said. "I loved living in it."

"I hope the new owners appreciate what we've put into it," Chet said.

Maureen nodded her head in sad agreement.

"The two hundred tulip bulbs I planted are going to look awfully pretty when they come up in the spring."

They had reached the point where they had to turn their backs on their little brick house. Chet climbed into the truck with Terry who was going to ride shotgun. Jennifer, Suzy and Maureen piled into the psychedelic van. They backed out of the drive-way with hardly a backwards glance, but they all had a sick feeling in their stomachs as they drove out of Dearborn for the last time.

They headed north on Telegraph and wound their way through the heavy holiday traffic to I-75. At the northbound entrance to the freeway Chet paused to look back at Maureen. He caught her eye and gave her a thumbs-up. She grinned and shot him a thumbs-up in return.

Chet leaned on the gas.

"Okay, Terry," he said. "Here goes nothing!"

He wheeled the rental truck onto the freeway with the determination of an immigrant headed for the promised land. Now he knew what it was like to pack up all one's worldly possessions and head off into the unknown. He hoped he would have the fortitude to survive the way the pioneers did. At least he wouldn't be facing Indians.

Chet looked over at Terry. The boy had crossed his fingers on both hands and was squeezing his eyes tightly shut.

"What are you wishing for?" Chet asked.

"Can't tell."

Terry finally released his fingers and opened his eyes.

"Good one?" Chet asked.

"All wishes are good," Terry said.

"Bet I can guess what it was."

"Don't, dad!" Terry said. "If you do it won't come true!"

"Okay," Chet said holding up his hand. "I'll shut up."

That was the first time Terry had ever called him dad, and Chet was flattered. He was only the boy's uncle by marriage but Terry had lived with them for the last three years. It was only natural that Terry should think of Chet and Maureen as his parents.

Yet for some reason Chet was reluctant to acknowledge the relationship formally. Whenever Maureen suggested adopting Terry he always found a good reason not to. For one thing, he felt strongly that Terry should keep his own name. It would be important that his identity not be swallowed up in theirs. Maureen never pressed the matter. She always seemed to understand his reluctance and let it go at that.

Terry touched Chet on the arm. When he had his attention he said, "Wishes can come true, can't they?"

Chet thought for a moment before answering and then nodded his head. A nod seemed a whole lot less committal than a straight answer.

3

After two and a half hours of nonstop driving they reached a junction outside Bay City and followed Highway 10 west. Twenty minutes later they came to Midland and stopped at one of the few restaurants that was open. By a stroke of luck they were able to get turkey and trimmings.

"This is better than eating at home," Maureen said, bravely ignoring the jellied cranberry sauce that still bore the imprint of the can.

Chet studied the dry drumstick he was chewing.

"At least you girls won't have to do the dishes," he said.

"And you guys won't fall asleep watching football," Jennifer said.

"We never watch football," Terry said. "We always watch a movie."

"I wonder if *Miracle on 34th Street* is on again?" Chet said. "I really didn't want to miss it."

"You can afford to miss it," Maureen said. "You've seen it a dozen times."

"Two dozen," Chet said. "And I hope to see it two dozen more."

"So do I," Terry said.

Maureen glanced nervously at Terry and then at Chet.

"Are we almost there?" she asked, quickly changing the subject.

"We're still an hour's drive away," Chet said.

"How come we haven't seen any snow yet?" Terry asked.

"There's plenty of time for snow," Maureen said. "It isn't December yet. When December comes we'll have snow up to our ears, and Jack Frost will be nipping at your noses."

She gave all their noses a tweak, including Chet's.

"I hope I like it," Terry said.

"What?" Maureen asked. "The snow?"

"The new house. It's going to be my last one, isn't it?"

Maureen and Chet exchanged glances and then looked at the girls. The girls hadn't picked up on Terry's remark.

"I'm sure you're going to love the new house," Maureen said quickly. "It's a grand old Michigan farmhouse with a great big porch and a swing and a parlor for entertaining. There'll be separate bedrooms too, for each of you."

"Good," Terry said. "I hate sleeping in the same room with girls."

"Can Suzy and me share the same room?" Jennifer asked.

"Suzy and I," Chet corrected.

"Yes," Maureen said with a tolerant smile for Chet's incessant correcting. "You *may* share the same room or you may have your own. There are six to choose from. Won't it be fun choosing? We can go skating on the lake too. We'll even be able to cut down a Christmas tree on our own property."

Maureen chattered on, trying valiantly to be convincing, but all she was doing was echoing what the realtor had said. Sight unseen, they had leased an old farmhouse on a lake near a small town. The house sounded exactly like what they needed to take them through the trying times ahead. But she was still apprehensive about what they would find when they got there.

Chet listened politely while he sipped his coffee. There was doubt in his eyes too but he kept it to himself. Maureen was thankful for that. Her own doubts were difficult enough to live with. The children, of course, were oblivious to everything but the excitement of this new adventure. She was thankful for that too.

❄ ❄ ❄

4

An hour later their little caravan turned down Mittenville's main drag. A white clapboard town hall guarded one end of the street while a white church with an imposing steeple defended the other.

"What a charming town," Maureen said to the girls. "It looks like nothing's changed in a hundred years."

"How boring," Suzy said.

"Isn't that a pretty church?" Maureen said. She could see candles inside and could pick out the faint harmonies of the choir. "Sounds wonderful, doesn't it?" She suddenly felt an aching loneliness for the little chapel in Greenfield Village.

"Is that the church we'll be going to?" Jennifer asked.

"I think so," Maureen said. "Don't you?"

"What religion is it?" Suzy asked.

"Does it matter?" Maureen said.

"It doesn't matter to God," Jennifer said with the

11

certainty of innocence. "That's why there are so many different kinds."

Maureen smiled to herself.

"Oh look," she said. "There's an old-fashioned dry goods store, and a dime store too."

"Do they sell dimes?" Suzy asked.

"No. They call it a dime store because in the olden days they used to sell lots of things for a dime."

"Can we go in?" Jennifer asked.

"We'll make a special trip into town next week," Maureen said. "But I don't think we'll be able to buy much for a dime."

At the intersection Chet rolled down the window and asked an old-timer for directions to Ontonagon. The old-timer gave him an odd look.

"Lake Ontonagon," Chet said, enunciating distinctly for the benefit of the old geezer. "How do we get there?"

Without a word, the old geezer swept his arm in a circle and jerked his thumb over his shoulder. Chet waved his thanks and looked back to see if Maureen was still following him. She was. Chet caught a glimpse of the old geezer staring at the van. He had his hands on his hips as if he refused to believe what he was seeing. Obviously, a van of many colors had never cruised through their fair streets before.

Chet followed the paved road until the pavement stopped. Then he followed the gravel until the gravel stopped. The road began to narrow until the

13

branches of the trees were scraping the sides of the truck. Chet glanced in his side view mirror and saw that even the smaller van was getting its share of abrasions.

"I wonder what these branches are doing to the artwork?" he said.

"Maybe we won't have to paint it," Terry said.

He sprang from his seat and pointed.

"There it is, dad!"

"There what is?"

"The road to Lake Ontonagon! You're going to miss it!"

Chet saw the old wooden sign just in time and wheeled the truck into a hard turn. It was all he could do to keep the overloaded vehicle from capsizing.

"I hope the furniture in back is enjoying the ride!" he said.

In the side-view mirror he could see that Maureen was managing to keep up. She kept craning her head as she strained for a first glimpse of their new home. In the seat beside her the twins were jumping up and down excitedly.

They came up over a hill and broke into a clearing just as the sun broke through the clouds. There in the distance, in a rambling grass meadow, glittered the mile-square lake called Ontonagon. Chet slowed down and pulled over so they could get a better look.

Flocks of mallards were skimming its surface while

droves of Canada geese waddled around its rim. Off in a stand of oaks, looking quite majestic in the bright sunlight, stood the three-story white farmhouse. It would be theirs for as long as they could afford the rent. And there were no other houses in sight so they would have all the privacy they wanted. It was all so very poetic it took Chet's breath away. Things didn't seem so dismal after all.

"Our new home," Chet said. "Not bad, huh?"

"There's no ice," Terry said flatly. "And no snow either."

"And I don't see any Christmas trees," Chet said. "But let's not sweat the details. I'm sure we'll get more than we bargained for."

Maureen pulled the van alongside and blasted her horn. Chet rolled down the window to say something but Maureen rolled right by.

"Let's go, dad!" Terry said. "They're going to beat us!"

Chet took his foot off the brake and floored the accelerator pedal. The truck lurched ahead like it was stuck in molasses. It rocked and rolled down the rutted road until it slowly picked up downhill momentum. Soon they were clipping along at a speed that must have been decidedly unsafe for that kind of vehicle on that kind of road. But Terry was laughing for the first time in a long time so Chet kept the pedal to the metal.

They caught up with the bouncing van and

stayed on its tail. The ground was flat and smooth so Chet decided to pass. He eased his wheels out of the rut, drew alongside the van and glanced over at Maureen. She was so intent on winning the race she wouldn't even look at him.

But the truck had used up all its power and Chet had to settle for careening into the front yard in a dead heat. It was only after they had jerked to a stop and their laughter subsided that they noticed the Sheriff's car parked in the driveway.

"Uh oh, the welcome wagon's here," Chet said to Terry. "Wait in the truck until I find out what's wrong."

5

The Sheriff played it cool as he watched Chet and Maureen climb down out of their vehicles. He held one hand on his holstered gun and used the other to scratch the head of the killer Doberman sitting in the front seat of his car.

Chet and Maureen walked up and stood there like a couple of wayward teenagers who couldn't keep from grinning at each other. The Doberman caught their scent and let out a nervous yelp. It became agitated and spun around a few times but stayed obediently inside the car.

The Sheriff looked up at them from his short height and smiled. But then he let his smile fall quickly away.

"I guess you quick-draws from the city couldn't get here fast enough," he said, his voice edged with the nasal twang of northern Michigan.

Maureen pawed at the ground with her foot. She wanted very much to look at the house but the house would have to wait until she finished negotiating.

17

"I'm afraid in our enthusiasm we drove a little too fast," she said. "But we were only endangering ourselves. That was pretty stupid since we have children with us."

She was being a little too candid to suit Chet so he gave her one of those looks that was supposed to shut her up. But she ignored him the way she always did.

"We were all belted in, and we're really safe drivers," Maureen went on. "Neither of us has any points on our licenses."

"I know," the Sheriff said.

"You know?" Chet said, surprised.

"What you do on your property is your business," the Sheriff said. Then he added ominously, "for the most part."

Maureen was pleased to hear that.

"That's very enlightened," she said.

"I try to keep an open mind," the Sheriff said. "At least until all the evidence is in."

"I'll remember that," Chet said and stuck out his hand. "We're the Alcots. My name is Chet and this chatty lady is Maureen."

They shook hands.

"Pleased to make your acquaintance," the Sheriff said. "You two married?"

"Of course we are," Maureen said. "Why do you ask?"

"We don't often see that in folks who come up

here from the city."

"Well, you sure see it in us," Chet said. "And your name is—?"

"Sheriff Jerome K. Hobbs," the Sheriff said with a little strut. "Eternally vigilant in the service of Justice. That's our creed. Thought it up all by myself."

"Then I'm pleased to make your acquaintance," Chet said. "Unless of course there's a problem."

"No problem," the Sheriff said. "I'm just doing you the courtesy of checking you in."

Chet went rigid and Maureen noticed it.

"Checking us in?" Chet said. "What's that supposed to mean?"

The Sheriff took out his notebook and flipped it open. Chet tried to see what he was looking at but the Sheriff turned his back on him the way a kid would.

"I thought this was a free country," Chet protested.

"It may be," the Sheriff said. "But this isn't a free *county.*"

Maureen didn't like the way things were going. When it came to civil liberties Chet could get on his high horse faster than Patrick Henry. Especially when his liberties were at issue. So she gave him her special version of the look that was supposed to shut him up. Only now it was he who ignored her.

"I don't know what's in your little book," Chet said, but we paid our rent six months in advance."

"That's good," the Sheriff said. "That means I won't have to chase you all over the state to collect."

Chet was astonished. "You mean you're the rent collector?"

"Nope. But I do run a pristine county." The Sheriff placed his heavy hand on Chet's shoulder. "Nobody is beyond the reach of the law in this part of Michigan." He suddenly adopted a pleasant tone. "Anyhow, you folks are moving into a money hole."

Maureen shot a glance at the house. "A what?"

"This old house is going to need a whole lot of repairs," the Sheriff said cheerfully. "That means you're going to be running up a whole lot of bills in my county. I just want to make sure your creditors get paid."

"We're not going to have creditors," Chet said. "It's up to the landlord to pay for repairs. That's the law."

"Not if you rented the place as is," the Sheriff grinned. "That's also the law."

Chet looked to Maureen for support but she just shrugged.

"The realtor said we could move right in," Maureen said.

"What little work needs to be done I can do myself," Chet said.

"Are you a licensed carpenter or plumber?" the Sheriff asked.

"Do I have to be for a few simple repairs?"

"Come with me," the Sheriff said.

He led the way up onto the porch and stood in the middle of it. He rocked back and forth on his feet until the groaning floorboards sounded like they were going to collapse.

"Hear that?" the Sheriff said. "Dry rot."

"Old farmhouses make lots of noise," Maureen said gamely. "It's part of their charm."

"Then this house has a lot of charm," the Sheriff said.

He walked up to the front door and gave it a shove. It started to creak open but fell off its hinges in mid-swing. Chet gave Maureen a despairing glance but she looked the other way.

"At least the kids won't be slamming the door," she said.

Her heart sank when she peeked inside and saw the wallpaper curling off the walls.

"Kids'll have to go to school," the Sheriff said. "That means the bus will have to come way out here to pick them up. That's a lot of added expense for the school district."

"I was planning on driving them," Maureen said. "If it matters."

"It matters," the Sheriff said. "My sister-in-law's the driver and gets paid by the kid. How many kids did you say you have?"

"We didn't!" Chet said.

Chet was beginning to sound pugnacious so

21

Maureen moved him safely out of the line of fire and waved the kids up onto the porch.

"We have three kids," she said and watched them charge out of their vehicles and run up the steps. "Suzy, Jennifer and Terry. Kids, say hello to Sheriff Hobbs."

"Hello, Sheriff!" the kids yelled in rapid fire.

"Pleased to meet you," the Sheriff said and patted them on the head as they tore past and ran inside.

"The twins are seven and the boy's eleven," Maureen said with pride. "They're our lucky numbers."

The Sheriff glanced in his notebook. "As we say in law enforcement, that don't compute."

"What don't?"

"You only have two kids." The Sheriff tapped his notebook ominously. "Two twin girls. Where'd the boy come from?"

Chet couldn't believe what he was hearing.

"What is this, the Gestapo?" he shouted. "Besides, two twins is redundant!"

The Sheriff was bewildered. "Two twins is what?"

"What concern is it of yours how many kids we have?" Chet said.

The Sheriff tucked his notebook into his hip pocket and took up an aggressive stance.

"I'll tell you what concern it is," he said with the swagger of authority. "We could have a kidnap case here, now couldn't we?"

"Terry is our nephew!" Chet said loudly and

deliberately. "He's staying with us for—well, for the time being!"

"I suppose you've got his parents' permission?" the Sheriff asked. "In writing?"

"The parents are dead," Chet said. "Isn't that in your little black book too?"

"No it isn't," the Sheriff said, suddenly contrite. "I'm sorry about that. But you shouldn't get so upset over routine inquiries. The only people who get upset are those who have something to hide."

"A totally flawed premise," Chet said.

"Is it really? Do *you* have something to hide?"

"No!" Chet almost yelled. "And there's nothing routine about this inquiry. What in blazes are you looking for?"

"Trouble before it starts," the Sheriff said. He held his hand up like a torch. "Eternal vigilance! That's what our creed calls for."

"Very commendable," Maureen said, desperately trying to alter the mood. "Do you have children too, Sheriff?"

"I do," the Sheriff said in another surprising change of attitude. "My lucky numbers are 32 and 34. You'll be meeting them soon."

"Oh? Why is that?"

"One's a licensed carpenter and plumber. The other's a licensed furnace man and mason."

"Keeps it all in the family, doesn't it?" Chet said with unveiled scorn.

The Sheriff reached into his pocket and drew out two business cards.

"You're welcome to call on my boys," he said amicably and held the cards out to Chet. "But your credit better be good. They're deputies too."

Maureen accepted the cards and passed them on to Chet.

"You don't have to worry about our credit," Chet said. He put the cards in his pocket and made a mental note to throw them away. "We always pay cash."

The Sheriff's eyes widened.

"Carry around a lot of cash, do you? Now isn't that interesting!"

❄ ❄ ❄

6

"We don't usually carry cash," Maureen said. "But we sold most of our belongings to come up here, so we're flush."

"Flush?" the Sheriff was intrigued. "Care to explain why you had to sell everything and get out of town fast?"

"It's a long story," Chet said. He was growing impatient with this bumpkin of a Sheriff and his Napoleonic complex. "I don't have the time or the inclination to tell it to you. It's getting late and the kids need to be fed and put to bed."

The Doberman started to whine. The Sheriff looked at the dog and then at the van. He stepped down off the porch and walked over to it.

"This amazing ve-hicle belong to you?" the Sheriff asked.

"Yes, why?" Chet said following him down.

"Dirty Harry's the best sniffer in these parts," the Sheriff said. "He don't go into heat for nothing."

"Oh my God!" Maureen said and put her hand to

her mouth.

The Sheriff picked up on that.

"You folks wouldn't be trafficking in a controlled substance, would you?"

"Up here?" Chet said with a silly grin. "Why on earth would anybody want to do that?"

"I don't know," the Sheriff said, "but they always do. Last bunch almost burned this house down. Had a van that looked just like yours."

"There are no drugs in our van," Chet said. "You can take my word for that."

"I do," the Sheriff said, his voice dripping with sarcasm. "But I'd like Dirty Harry to see for himself. To satisfy his canine curiosity, of course."

"No way," Chet said. "The Constitution protects us against unreasonable search and seizure."

"Seizure of what?"

"Nothing!"

"I can get a search warrant awful fast."

"You'll need probable cause."

Maureen went up to Chet.

"Honey," she said, "please stop. There's no point to all this."

"*He's* the one who should stop," Chet said indignantly. "*I'm* the one who's in the right!"

The Sheriff gave a sharp whistle and Dirty Harry bounded out of the car. He galloped over to the van and circled it frantically. His tail wagged stiffly while his nose sniffed at every crevice. Every once in a while he yelped and pawed at the car.

"There's your probable cause," the Sheriff said. "That van's *dirty.*"

"Better get a search warrant," Chet said. "Everything we have is in that van, and you're not going to get my permission to let your mutt rip through it."

The Sheriff was more disappointed than he was angry.

"Is that the way it's going to be?" he said plaintively.

"Maybe you should just tell the Sheriff where we got the van," Maureen said as reasonably as she could. "That should put an end to all this."

"That's not the point," Chet said. "This is an outrageous example of unlawful search and seizure. He shouldn't be able to get away with it."

"Your husband a lawyer, ma'am?" the Sheriff asked Maureen.

"No!" she said with annoyance. "But he sure knows how to act like one!"

"I'm not acting like anybody," Chet said with the precision of an editor. "I'm a private citizen who's insisting on his constitutionally guaranteed rights."

Maureen decided this ridiculous duel had gone far enough.

"We're not transporting drugs," she said to the Sheriff. "We're not the kind of people who would do that for money."

27

"You'd be surprised what nice people will do for money," the Sheriff said. "Especially at this time of year. Christmas brings out the best in folks."

"We bought this van at a police auction," Maureen explained. "It used to belong to somebody who sold drugs, but he was caught and sent to jail."

"The residue," Chet finally volunteered. "That must be what Dirty Harry smells."

"The what?"

"Some angel dust must have fallen in the cracks."

The Sheriff squinted at Chet.

"Sounds farfetched to me," he said. He hitched up his gun belt and cleared his throat. "But since it's Thanksgiving Day, I'm prepared to give you the benefit of the doubt."

He bent down and ran his hand along the sill of the van. Then he rubbed his fingers together and sniffed them with practised expertise.

"Reasonable doubt it is," he said. "You get the benefit."

The Sheriff snapped his fingers. Dirty Harry ran back to the car and hopped in through the window.

"But if you're not trafficking in controlled substances the way your van says you are, what are you doing here?"

"We came for the snow," Maureen said.

"Skiing? There's no skiing here," the Sheriff said. "You should have gone to Gaylord or Boyne."

"We're not interested in skiing. All we want is

snow. Ontonagon gets more snow than any place in the Lower Peninsula. We looked it up."

"It should," the Sheriff said. "Ontonagon's in the Upper Peninsula, four hundred miles north of here."

"What?" Maureen said and her mouth fell open. It was a decidedly unladylike gesture but she didn't care. "What do you mean it's four hundred miles north of here?"

"Not unusual in Michigan for two places to have the same name," the Sheriff said. "There's Houghton Lake in the next county, and Houghton city in the U. P."

Maureen blanched. "That was our second choice!"

"As for snow," the Sheriff went on, "Lake Ontonagon hardly gets any. Hardly gets any rain either. This year we're lucky there's a lake there at all."

"This is devastating," Maureen said. "How could we make a mistake like that?"

"Search me," the Sheriff said and walked back to his car. "Every dumb-bunny in the state knows that."

Chet watched dumbfounded as the Sheriff got into his car, started the engine and shifted into gear.

"Have a happy Thanksgiving!" the Sheriff called out and pulled away with a short sassy blast of his siren.

The kids tried to open the upstairs window to see what all the fuss was but the sash came loose and tumbled out. Chet blithely watched it fall to the ground and smash into pieces.

"What did we do to the gods to deserve this?" he asked Maureen, not really expecting an answer. "We sold our wonderful house and beautiful Bimmer and moved north just so the kid's wish could come true. And what happens? We end up here where they've never even heard of snow—"

"He didn't exactly say that, dear," Maureen interjected.

"—harassed by a paranoid Sheriff who happens to be a megalomaniac! With a killer dog that's psychotic! And a hundred-year-old house that's falling down around our ears!"

"It isn't really that bad. Is it?"

"I think it is. We've got grounds for a law suit. In fact we've got grounds for suing the whole county!"

"I think we need a fresh perspective," Maureen said in that soothing voice she always trotted out at times like this.

"I don't need a fresh perspective," Chet said, allowing himself to be led back up onto the porch. "I happen to like the one I've got."

She steered him over to the swing that was hanging from the porch ceiling by two rusty chains. She sat him down on the wooden slats and gave the swing a shove. The squeaking reminded her of the old swing set they left behind in Dearborn.

Chet looked up at her. "What do you think I am?

A kid?"

She sat down beside him and took a deep breath as she took in the grandeur of the sky and the lake, and the clouds and the trees.

"Isn't this a pretty view?" she said.

Chet grunted.

"That lake must get its water from somewhere," she said. "It's so perfectly blue."

"It's probably the cesspool for Mittenville," Chet said and extended his legs the way a kid would. "Ontonagon Lake!" he said shaking his head. "How could I have been so stupid?"

"I was the one who was stupid," Maureen said and extended her legs alongside his.

They listened to the swing creak and watched the golden sun slide into the icy blue water. Chet relented and put his arm around her the way he did when times were tough, which they always seemed to be lately.

"We were stupid together," he said. "Let's not sweat it, okay?"

She smiled gamely and the tears welled up again. Chet wiped them away with his thumb.

"It'll be all right," he said. "You and the kids get the sleeping bags out of the van while I turn the heat on in the house. Then we can figure out how to play these lousy cards we've just been dealt."

At precisely that moment the hooks pulled out of the ceiling and the swing came crashing down with

Chet and Maureen still in it. Chet started to say something awful but Maureen put her fingers over his mouth. She raised them only long enough to kiss him on the lips.

"Dry rot," she said and started to giggle.

Chet's face creased into a reluctant smile.

"Aren't we a couple of idiot fools!" he said.

"Idiot fools?" Maureen said. "That's redundant."

They both giggled, pretty soon uncontrollably, and then rolled in each other's arms. Behind them the lake was being magically transformed into molten gold.

7

Chet backed the van up to the porch and crawled inside. He was passing the sleeping bags out to Maureen when Terry and the twins came up.

"There's a man in the house," Jennifer said.

Maureen abruptly stopped what she was doing. "A man? Where?"

"In the attic," Suzy said.

"I was up there," Terry said. "But I didn't see anybody."

"Well we did!" Jennifer said indignantly. "We think the house is haunted."

Terry was unimpressed and climbed up on the rail to sulk.

"Is that possible?" Maureen asked Chet. "That there's a man in the house?"

"The place does look abandoned," Chet said and climbed out of the van. "So it is possible. Where was he and what was he doing?"

"He was in the attic," Suzy said.

"He wasn't doing anything," Jennifer said. "Just standing there."

Chet picked up a heavy metal flashlight and smacked it in the palm of his hand. "Let's check it out," he said.

He stepped over the fallen front door and led the way into the house. Maureen and the kids stayed close behind. It was already dark inside so he had to sweep the walls with a beam of light until he found the light switch. He pushed one of the old-fashioned round buttons and a dim bulb in the overhead fixture flickered on.

They were standing in the dilapidated foyer. The wallpaper was torn and peeling, and the floor tiles were loose. A pair of closed sliding doors confronted them from both sides while at the far end a staircase hunkered in the darkness. There was also the unmistakably sweet stench of old marijuana smoke.

"Where would you like to start?" Chet said.

"In here," Maureen said, and cautiously opened the sliding doors on the left. "This should be the parlor."

Chet flashed the light inside.

"Nobody in there," he said. "We can go right in."

Maureen found the switch and turned the lights on.

"Look at this gorgeous chandelier," she said. "The crystal acts like a prism and scatters shards of colored light all over the walls."

Chet was concentrating on the fireplace where he found remnants of furniture that had been burned. Not a good sign. But then there weren't any good signs.

"We can light a fire and spend the night here if the furnace doesn't work," he said. "Which it probably doesn't."

"Goody!" Jennifer said. "I hope it doesn't work."

Maureen walked to the back of the room and peered through the grimy glass of the French doors.

"The porch goes all the way around the house," she said. "It's wonderful."

Chet opened a pair of doors to an adjacent room and turned on the light. Maureen came up behind him and looked over his shoulder.

"A dining room with a bay window," she said in hushed reverence and went in. "I've always wanted a separate dining room!"

She ran her fingers across the red flocked wallpaper and stroked the velvet drapes that hung from the crooked valance. Chet moved quietly across the room, pushed open a swinging door and peeked inside.

"This has to be the kitchen," he said and turned on the light.

It was a huge farm kitchen with an ancient wood-burning stove right in the middle of the room. The walls were covered with cupboards but the doors were warped and wouldn't stay shut. Maureen was undismayed.

"I love it!" she said. "A little shelf paper will do wonders."

Chet turned on the faucets that protruded from the porcelain steel sink but nothing came out.

"There must be a pump somewhere that has to be switched on," he said.

Jennifer opened a door. "What's in here, Mom?"

Maureen peeked inside. "The pantry," she said. "We could store a whole supermarket in there if we had to."

"We may have to," Chet said. "The A&P is no longer five minutes away."

Terry opened another door and was greeted by a yawning black hole.

"Where does this go?" he said backing away.

"To the basement," Chet said. "Coming down?"

"I'll wait here," Terry said. "It's scary down there."

"We'll wait here too," Maureen said and gathered the twins around her.

Chet turned on the light and descended slowly into the small dank cellar. He shined his light into the dark corners to make sure nobody was there. Nobody was. The cellar was dominated by a coal-burning furnace that had been converted to oil. The tank showed half full so he flipped on the switch. Nothing happened. Nothing ever happened in this house.

In the far corner stood what looked like a water pump with an electrical cord dangling from it. Chet plugged the cord into an outlet and jumped back in surprise when the pump thundered into life. The pipes vibrated loudly and upstairs the kitchen faucets coughed and sputtered.

"Water!" Maureen called down.

"Brown water!" Terry said.

"Let it run until it clears!" Chet called back.

The softener and the electric water heater appeared to be in good shape so he turned them on too. Then he took one last look around and wondered if anybody was buried there. When he was certain at least a dozen people were, he swept the cobwebs out of his hair and hurried back upstairs.

"What's it like?" Maureen asked.

"No laundry room." Chet said. "Just a zillion canning jars."

He turned off both faucets even though the water was still running slightly brown.

"We have to have a laundry room," Maureen said looking around the kitchen. "Where could it be?"

"I'll bet it's in town," Chet said.

He stepped into the foyer and turned on the thermostat. Nothing happened again.

"You're in luck, Jenn," Chet said. "Looks like the furnace doesn't work."

"Call the furnace repair man," Maureen said. "The Sheriff gave us his card."

"I'll have to. Where's the telephone?"

"There isn't one," Terry said. "We already looked."

"We'll have to build a fire!" Jennifer said excitedly.

"Won't it be fun?" Maureen said.

"Fires are fun!" Suzy said.

"I just remembered the crucial ingredient," Chet said. "Did anybody bring an axe?"

"No," Maureen said. "But I did bring electric blankets."

Chet turned to the kids.

"Let that be a lesson to you," he said. "Always remember to bring the essentials."

Suzy opened the sliding doors on the right side of the foyer.

"Can we go in here?" she said and started to enter the room.

Maureen drew her back. "Let Daddy go in first, dear."

Chet swept the room with his flashlight and then Maureen and the kids went in.

"This must have been the library," Maureen said. "It'll make a marvelous study."

"And there's another fireplace," Suzy said. "We can build a fire in here too."

"If we can find some wood," Terry reminded her.

Chet tousled Terry's head.

"So far we haven't found anything yet, have we sport?"

"Or anybody," Terry said.

"We haven't been upstairs yet," Jennifer said reproachfully.

"Well?" Chet said indicating the staircase with a grand sweep of his hand. "Shall we venture upstairs?"

Maureen held the kids back and, with a grand sweep of her own, gave Chet the honor of leading the way.

8

At the top of the stairs they found five bedrooms that looked pretty much alike. All had over-head lights that came on with a pull chain, and all had large closets that would have made excellent hiding places.

"There's more closet space up here than we had in our entire house," Chet said, dutifully inspecting every one.

"More windows too," Maureen said as she looked out on the darkening countryside. "We're pretty iso-lated."

"That's what we wanted."

The kids found a huge linen closet in the hall and held the door open for Chet. He shined his light inside.

"You could hide a boy scout pack in here," he said.

"Or their linens," Maureen said looking in over his shoulder. "We'll use every inch."

They continued down the hall and found a door

that led into a large bathroom. The floor-length mirrors along one wall were miraculously unbroken. Along the other wall there was a pedestal sink and an old-style cast iron tub. An adjoining door led to another bathroom of equal size. This one had a shower stall in place of the tub.

"These bathrooms are fabulous," Chet said. "If they work."

He flushed one toilet, then went back and flushed the other. They both worked flawlessly despite the color of the water.

"I'm beginning to like this place," he said.

"You like it because you think you're going to have your own private bathroom," Maureen said. "Just remember, there are five of us."

"Where's the other bedroom?" Chet asked. "We rented six."

"Up here," Terry said and opened a narrow door in a corner of the hall.

"That's where the man is," Suzy said.

Chet came up and looked into the blackness. "Where's the light switch?"

"There isn't one," Terry said.

"Nice," Chet said. He turned on his flashlight and shined it up the narrow stairs. "Everybody wait here."

"Oh no you don't," Maureen said. "We're coming with you."

They marched up in single file behind Chet. The

attic was typical—dusty and cold with exposed rafters. The only light came from the window the kids had knocked out.

"There's no bedroom up here," Maureen said. "We've been had!"

"Have you just now figured that out?" Chet said. He shined his light into the dark corners. "There's not even a stick of old furniture. It's probably all been burned for heat."

"Where did you see the man?" Maureen asked.

"Right there," Suzy said pointing to a spot in the middle of the floor.

Chet got down on one knee and flared the light horizontally across the floorboards. Despite the unevenness of the planks he was able to highlight the footprints the kids had left in the heavy layer of dust.

"I can see your footprints," he said. "But not any big ones."

"That's a relief," Maureen said.

"But we saw him," Jennifer said. "Standing right here."

She walked over and stood on the spot.

"Honey," Maureen said, "there are no footprints there but yours."

"Ghosts don't leave footprints," Jennifer said.

"Ghosts?" Maureen glanced at Chet.

"This house is haunted," Suzy said with finality.

"Well if it's haunted," Chet said, "let's be glad Mr.

Ghost lives up here. Right now we'd better go downstairs and find some wood. It's getting dark and I think we're going to have a chilly night."

Terry and the twins scrambled downstairs followed by Chet. Maureen lingered for a last look around. She had always wondered whether ghosts really existed, and if she would remain calm if one ever presented itself to her.

Suddenly she felt a chill surge through the room. Every hair on her body felt like it was standing on end. She spun around but saw nothing. Yet she was sure she could sense another presence. She spun around again. Yes, it was there—a spirit without form or substance. Or was it just her overactive imagination? She shuddered slightly.

"Wait for me!" she called out and scurried down the stairs after them.

9

C het went off scavenging for wood while Maureen climbed into the van and hauled out the sleeping bags and the electric blankets. She assembled them into five sets and dragged three into the parlor for the kids. The other two she put in the library for herself and for Chet.

The twins immediately began arranging their sleeping accommodations on one side of the fireplace. Terry set up his on the other side. An unoccupied no-man's-land lay in between.

Maureen went back to the van and foraged for towels and washcloths. She brought them out along with Chet's shaving gear and her own essential hair dryer and make-up kit. Then she trundled everything into the house and started to carry it all upstairs.

Maureen stopped on the first step and looked up. It seemed awfully dark and forbidding up there so she stacked everything in neat piles at the foot of the stairs. It wouldn't be needed until morning anyway, she told herself.

Chet struggled in with an arm load of wood and let it clatter to the floor. Maureen picked up a dry old board.

"This is perfect for burning," she said. "Where did you find it?"

"Plenty of loose stuff on the other side of the lake," Chet said out of breath. "All we have to do is get it here."

He stacked the wood in the fireplace and Terry lit a match.

"Hold it," Chet said. "We'd better open the damper first or the smoke will choke us out."

He reached up into the chimney and gave the steel handle a pull. Soot sifted down. Suddenly something black flew out and flashed past their faces with a draft that blew out the match. It fluttered wildly around the parlor while the twins covered their heads with their arms and screamed.

"What is it?" Maureen cried, adding her screams to theirs.

"It's a bat," Chet said from his position on the floor. "Trying to find a way out of this noisy, scary place."

The bat circled the ceiling and sent out squeals of sonar as it searched for an opening. It found the door to the dining room and darted inside. It flew up against the drape in front of the bay window and hung there, the claws at the tip of its folded web

45

wings dug deeply into the fabric.

"Let's kill it!" Terry said and jumped up with a big piece of wood.

"We try not to kill living things," Chet said. "Leave that to God."

"How are we supposed to get rid of it without killing it?" Maureen asked.

Chet motioned her to be still and warily approached the bat.

"It sure is ugly," he said. "One of God's practical jokes."

The sinister-looking creature was huge. Its ears were pointed, and white fangs protruded from its snout. The sides of its rat-like body pulsated furiously.

"It's probably more frightened of us than we are of it," Chet said.

"Not true!" Maureen said. "Bats carry rabies. I'm getting the kids out of here."

She shooed them into the foyer.

"I want to stay and watch," Terry said and slipped back in.

"He can stay if he stands behind me," Chet said.

Terry got behind Chet, and Maureen ducked behind the sliding doors.

"Be careful," she said and closed the doors. "Let us know when it's safe to come back in."

Chet picked up a small stick, slid it behind the drape and unlatched the window. He raised the sash and twisted the drape so the bat was facing out. Then he jerked the drape twice and the bat took off into the night.

"Nothing to it," Chet said and closed the window.

Terry ran to the doors and slid them apart.

"You can come back in!" he said. "The bat is gone!"

"How did you do it?" Maureen asked.

"Nothing to it," Terry said. "We opened the window and the bat flew out."

"You're a very brave young man," Maureen said. "Now if you can get the fire going too, we can all get ready for bed."

Terry lit another match and soon the dry wood was blazing. Then he and Chet went into the library and built another one just like it, this time without incident. They also raised the fallen door in the foyer and propped two pieces of wood against it to keep it up.

"It's actually beginning to feel warm in here," Maureen said. "And civilized!"

When the kids were nestled all snug in their sleeping bags, she turned off the light. The room glowed with the cheery warmth of the fire.

"Do you think Mr. Ghost will visit us down here?" Suzy asked.

"There aren't any ghosts," Terry said. "Just like there isn't any Santa Claus."

47

"There is too a Santa Claus," Jennifer said.

"Only kids believe in Santa Claus," Terry said.

Maureen knelt down beside him. "I'm not a kid and I believe in him."

Terry glanced up at Chet.

"Do you believe in Santa Claus, dad?"

Chet hesitated. He could tell from the way Maureen was looking up at him that she wanted him to lie.

"I don't know what I believe in," he said.

"Nice," Maureen said and gave him a disgusted look.

Suzy said, "If you believe in Santa Claus, mom, does that mean you believe in ghosts too?"

"I don't know, honey," Maureen said. "I've never seen a ghost."

"You will if Mr. Ghost comes down while we're sleeping."

"You don't have to worry about that," Chet said. "Ghosts are like bats. They're afraid of people too."

"How come you know so much about ghosts?" Maureen asked. "Especially since you don't believe in them?"

Chet shrugged. "Maybe living here will make me a believer in a lot of things."

They said good night to the kids, closed the sliding doors to the parlor and went into the library where the fire was burning. Maureen unrolled a sleeping bag while Chet looked out the window.

Outside, darkness had fallen like a heavy cloak. Stars twinkled through breaks in the clouds. A few flakes of snow tumbled out of the night sky and floated down onto the barren ground.

"It's starting to snow," Chet said. "Maybe this is the beginning of our white Christmas."

Maureen joined him at the window.

"Good!" she said. "I hope that nasty old Sheriff was wrong and it snows all night until we're knee-deep in it. I want Terry to get his Christmas wish so bad!"

Chet kissed her on the forehead.

"He will," he said. "Don't worry about it." He looked around. "What did you do with the other sleeping bag?"

"Left it rolled up. Why?"

"Where are you going to sleep?"

"In yours," she said coyly. "If there's room."

Chet grinned. "There's always room for you."

They got undressed and crawled in together. Maureen snuggled up next to him.

"Isn't this fun?" she said.

"Why didn't we ever try this at home?" he said with awakened interest.

She nuzzled her nose into his neck.

"I love you so much, darling," she said. "Thank you for doing this."

"Doing what? Letting you sleep in my sleeping bag?"

"You know what I mean."

Chet grunted. "You're the one who's making the big sacrifice," he said. "You used to have a cute little house with a dishwasher and a laundry room and a smooth-top range. You even had a furnace that worked. Now all you've got is this old house, complete with bats and ghosts and a front door that doesn't open."

"That's all right," Maureen said. "As long as I've got you and the kids, I've got everything."

10

Chet awakened in the middle of the night. He could feel the cold air clawing at his nose. He raised his head and looked at the fire. It had nearly burned out. There was no escaping his fate. He'd have to crawl out of his warm sleeping bag, tippy-toe across the icy floor and put more wood on the fire.

Maureen stirred when she felt him getting out.

"Where are you going?" she asked without entirely coming around.

"To feed the fire," he grumbled. "I thought we were long past feedings in the middle of the night."

"Hurry back," Maureen said and buried herself more deeply in the sleeping bag. "I'm freezing."

"You should try it out here," Chet said. He was shivering over his entire body.

He tugged on his pants, grabbed what wood was left and put it on the fire. He blew some ash away and the new stuff quickly ignited. Then he tottered across the drafty foyer and into the dark parlor

51

where the fire had burned out completely.

He found some more wood and stacked it in the fireplace. Then he struck a match and watched it flare brilliantly. He saw something out of the corner of his eye and looked around. The dim shadow of a man was standing in front of the French doors. The man appeared to be dressed in a white gown of some kind.

The match flickered out. Chet struck another and held it over his head. Now there was nobody there. He let the match burn out and struck another. Nothing. Whatever was there had to have been a sleep-induced hallucination.

He touched the match to the kindling and fanned the tiny flame until it engulfed the wood. He warmed his hands over the fire and looked over his shoulder again. The flickering flames were illuminating the parlor and part of the dining room. The kids were fast asleep in their sleeping bags, but there was nobody else there.

Chet went to the French doors and tried them. They were locked. He went into the dining room and felt for the latch on the bay window. It was locked too. He was going to go into the kitchen but decided the trip in bare feet wasn't worth it. He went back into the library and crawled into his sleeping bag.

Maureen enveloped him with her nice warm body.

"You're cold!" she mumbled, managing to communicate her vexation even in her sleep.

Chet said nothing. He just lay there, eyes open, watching and waiting. Fatigue finally overcame his curiosity and he fell fast asleep.

11

The first thing Maureen did when she got up was look outside. There was no snow. Fog was lying heavily across the water and in the trees. That meant a warm front was moving in. They might even have rain before the day was out. Then if it turned cold, who knew?

She dressed hurriedly. Inside it was certainly cold enough to snow. The fires in both rooms had gone out and she couldn't start them again because there was no more wood. She went out through a window in the foyer and retrieved the electric coffee maker and a can of coffee from the van. She took these into the kitchen and ran the water until it was clear. Then she put on the coffee and went back for the rest of the food and her ultimate weapon: the electric frying pan!

The aroma of cooking bacon finally roused Chet. He opened his eyes and for a moment couldn't believe where he was. It had to be heaven. When the door opened and Maureen came in with a mug of steaming coffee he was sure it was heaven.

"Time to get up," she said. "It's nearly seven."

Chet groaned. "Nobody in heaven gets up at seven!"

He wrapped his hands around the hot mug and sipped some of the steamy brew.

"How much snow did we get?"

"Tons," Maureen said. "Of fog. The thermometer outside the kitchen registers forty-three degrees."

"Forty-three?" Chet slumped back down. "Isn't it ever going to get cold?"

"It's cold enough," Maureen said. "We're out of wood and the kids won't get out of their sleeping bags. They're eating breakfast in bed."

Chet stared at her. "You really know how to spoil them, don't you?"

"The same way I spoil you," she said and left him dopily sipping his coffee.

Chet gradually shifted his brain into drive. He would eat first, he thought, because he was famished. Then he would shower and shave—in brown water if he had to because he felt so scuzzy. Then he'd see if he could get the furnace running. But first he'd have to close up the hole in the attic where the window—

He sat up straight. Something unusual had happened in the middle of the night. That is, if it had happened at all. He had gotten up, that much was certain. The floor was an ice rink. And he had put more wood on the fire. Both fires. He remembered that too. And he had struck a match. More than one, in fact. That was when he had seen *the man in white!*

Or had he seen anything? What kind of a man would dress in white? Especially in a gown of white? If that wasn't a sleep-induced hallucination, then it was a bad dream. Weird combinations like that came along only in dreams.

Chet shaved, showered and wolfed down the best breakfast he'd ever had.

"What did you do differently?" he asked Maureen. "It tastes unusually great!"

" 'Tis the seasoning," she said smugly. "I added a little ice-cold country air."

Re-energized, Chet made four trips to the lake for wood and got both fires roaring again. Then he took out his tools and went up into the attic. He looked around for something to cover the missing window but all he could find were the boards on the floor.

He pried up a half-dozen of the short ones and started nailing them across the opening. He was halfway through when he heard a truck drive up. He looked through the opening and saw a van in the driveway with *Delmar's Furnace Repair & Masonry* on its side. A man and a woman got out. From above Chet could see Maureen come down off the porch to greet them.

"This is providential," he heard her say. "We

wanted to call you but we have no phone."

"Not quite providential, ma'am," the man said. "Sheriff Hobbs sent us over. The name's Delmar and this here's the wife. Wanda can help you get the kitchen up and running while I take care of the furnace."

"Delmar and Wanda Hobbs, I presume?" Maureen said.

"Same as the Sheriff," Delmar said proudly.

"How did you know our furnace wasn't working?"

"It never is," Delmar grinned.

They walked up onto the porch and out of Chet's sight.

Chet returned to putting up the last few boards when he heard one of the kids come into the attic.

"Hold this board for me," he said without turning around. "I just dropped my nail."

He bent down to pick up the nail and saw that there was nobody in the room with him. He looked up at the board. It seemed to be holding itself up.

"What's going on here?" he said in a surly tone of voice.

The board dropped out of the opening and fell into his hands. Chet felt the hackles on his neck rise. It was as if an invisible being were standing next to him.

"Who are you?" Chet said, and when he heard himself speak he realized how ridiculous he sounded.

He put the last board over the opening and hesitated. On impulse he said, "Hold this for me." Then he took his hands away. The board fell to the floor.

"Thanks," Chet said sourly.

He picked up the board and nailed it in place all by himself. Then he went downstairs in time to see Delmar coming up from the basement.

"Howdy," Delmar said with a gap-toothed grin and held out his hand. "Name's Delmar, and I just got your furnace going."

"So fast?" Chet said. He was still shaking the man's hand when the blower kicked on. "What did you do to it?"

"If I told you," Delmar said with an even wider grin, "you wouldn't need me."

"Stove's going too," Maureen said. "Mrs. Hobbs showed me how to load the wood to get the right draft."

"Name's Wanda," Mrs. Hobbs said and shook Chet's hand. "Nothin' to it when you've got burnin' wood this good."

"That's great," Chet said. "Because there's piles of it on the other side of the lake."

Wanda and Delmar exchanged glances.

"There's an old Chippewa burial ground there," Wanda said. "The graves are shallow with wooden dog houses built over them so they could put food inside to feed the dead spirits. That be where you got it?"

Chet was horrified. "You mean we've been burning holy wood?"

"Didn't mean no disrespect, did you?" Delmar said.

"Absolutely not!" Chet said. "Should I take the wood back?"

"That burial ground's mighty old," Wanda said. "And the nearest Chippewa reservation's forty miles south. Doubt they'll be needing it."

Delmar grinned broadly. "Learn something every day, don't you?"

Chet nodded and looked guiltily at Maureen.

"I see your front door needs a new jamb," Delmar said. "Brother Lester's bound to have one."

"I'm not surprised," Chet said. "How do we get in touch with Brother Lester?"

Delmar looked at his watch.

"He's just getting off duty. Should be here any minute."

Terry came bounding in. "Want me, Mom?"

"You need to take your—" Maureen hesitated. "Your vitamins, hon."

She opened a bottle of blue-striped capsules and gave one to Terry. Terry swallowed it with a glass of water and was gone as fast as he had come in.

"Odd color for vitamins," Wanda said, staring at the bottle. "Odd name, too—AZT."

Maureen put the bottle in the cupboard and closed the door but the door wouldn't stay closed.

"Terry's a hemophiliac," she said. "He needs special medication."

"Is that serious?" Delmar said. "The boy looks peaked."

"He was born without the protein that makes blood clot," Chet said. "A small cut could make him bleed to death."

"Heard of that," Wanda said. "The curse of kings."

"Sorry about that," Delmar said. He rapped his knuckles on the cupboard door. "Lester can take care of this too while he's here."

"If we can afford it," Chet said digging for his wallet. "How much are we into you for already?"

"Two dollars, to keep it legal."

Chet looked up in surprise.

"Two dollars? Is that all?"

"We'd do it free just to be neighborly," Delmar said. "The Sheriff says the two dollars helps with the tax man."

"That's very good of you," Chet said and handed him the two dollars. "You're sure this is enough?"

Delmar grinned again. "Too much can be as bad as too little."

"Never had to worry about getting too much," Wanda said sullenly.

They walked into the foyer and stepped through the window onto the porch.

"Think it'll snow for Christmas?" Chet asked as they watched the odd couple walk down to their van.

"Can't remember our last white Christmas," Wanda said, still sullen.

Delmar took off his cap and scratched his head.

"Sheriff bought three fancy new snowmobiles four or five years ago," he said. "Haven't had enough of the white stuff to take those suckers out for a test run. Makes the Sheriff kind of ornery this time of year."

"That explains a lot," Chet said.

Delmar pointed to Chet's van.

"Handsome ve-hicle you got there," he said. "Be glad to take 'er off your hands if you decide to sell."

"If I do I'll let you know," Chet said.

"Take 'er easy!" Delmar said, and he and Wanda climbed into their van and drove away.

"Nice people," Chet said after they'd gone.

"You say that like you're surprised."

"Aren't you? After Sheriff Hobbs and his killer dog?"

12

T hey had just gone into the house when another van drove up. This one had *Lester's Carpentry and Plumbing* written all over it. A man and a woman got out, and Chet and Maureen knew they were in for an instant replay. They went out to greet their visitors.

"Saw Delmar's truck leaving," the man said. "Reckon you know who I am."

"None other than the famous Lester Hobbs," Chet said.

"Ain't so famous as Mildred's pies," Lester said and helped his wife up the steps.

Mildred was carrying something under a brown checked napkin.

"Wanda bring you her pecan pie?" she asked Maureen darkly.

"No," Maureen said. "She didn't bring anything."

"Must have had a failure," Mildred said, her face lighting up. "She won't take that pie anywhere unless it's perfect."

Mildred removed the napkin and passed a huge cherry pie to Maureen.

"This pie is perfect," she said with finality.

"Thank you," Maureen said and showed the pie to Chet. "Isn't it fabulous?"

"It's all in the lard," Mildred said. "Wanda thinks she can make a decent crust without lard."

"Won't you come in and have some coffee?" Maureen said. "I'd love to know how you get your crust so golden. Is that in the lard too?"

"No it ain't," Mildred said and smiled crookedly. "It's all in the knowin' how."

Chet walked over to Lester.

"Don't Mildred and Wanda get along?"

"Famously," Lester said. "They're sisters." He jerked his head at Chet's van. "Good-lookin' vehicle. Want to sell 'er?"

"Not just yet," Chet said. "You interested?"

"Is Delmar?"

"Seemed to be."

"Then for sure I am."

Lester went to the rear of his van and opened both doors.

"Got a whole new front entrance for you," he said. "Want to give me a hand to haul 'er out?"

"How much is this going to cost?"

"How much did Delmar charge for what he did?"

"Two dollars," Chet said. "But he didn't do much."

"Did he get the furnace running?"

"In two minutes. All he had to do was jiggle a wire or something."

"Why didn't you jiggle it?" Lester asked.

"Didn't know what to jiggle, or how to jiggle it."

"I rest my case."

Lester pulled the door jamb out of the van. He ran his hand lovingly over the wood.

"There's no way I can install this beauty for two dollars," he said. "Costs a lot more than that just to buy it."

"Maybe I can get the landlord to pay for it," Chet said with little enthusiasm for the idea.

Lester shook his head.

"No chance of that," he said. "Are you going to take up the other end or just stand there?"

Chet grabbed the other end and helped Lester carry it over to the porch.

"How much does something like this cost?"

"This jamb came out of a house that was being tore down," Lester said.

"So it isn't new," Chet quickly added.

"Better than new. It's solid walnut. Nicely dried out. No warpin' or crackin'."

"So how much?"

"Set you back twenty dollars. With installation it could come to—thirty dollars easy?"

Lester watched Chet for his reaction.

"You're kidding," Chet said. "How can you guys make a living charging so little?"

"First visit's neighborly," Lester said. "Second time is strictly business."

"No cherry pie, huh?"

"Let's get this door fixed," Lester said. "Then I can tend to whatever else needs doin' at first-visit rates. This place is sure a mess."

"I'll say," Chet said. "I wonder who the landlord is and why he let it go to the dogs?"

"Sheriff's the landlord," Lester said and went back to the van to get his tools.

Chet let the information sink in. To be sure he had heard right, he followed Lester and said, "Did you say your father is the landlord?"

"Sheriff's the landlord," Lester said again. "Even though he's our pa we don't ever call him anything but Sheriff. He's got a thing about that."

"I'll bet he does," Chet said.

He went over to the porch steps and sat down with a thump.

The Sheriff's the landlord! What could possibly happen next?

13

That first Sunday Maureen insisted the children get dressed for church. She also insisted that Chet put on a tie and go with them even though he had a dozen excellent excuses not to. There were beds to set up, pictures to hang, the television set to connect, furniture to arrange—

"You're going," Maureen said sternly. "First impressions are important and I want ours to be positive."

"I know they're important," Chet said. "I don't want that pastor to think I'm going to become a permanent member of his flock."

"I wish you'd have a better attitude about that," Maureen said. "The kids are bound to pick up your cynicism."

"Why won't they pick up your piety?"

"You know why," Maureen said. "Wickedness is always more attractive than godliness."

They drove into town as the perfect devout family. And when they strolled up Main Street to that

wonderful white church it seemed as if everybody in Mittenville knew who they were.

"How come everybody knows our name?" Jennifer asked.

"Small towns know everybody and everything, dear," Maureen said.

"Let that be a lesson to you," Chet added.

The Reverend and Mrs. Hipwood were standing in the portico to welcome them along with a phalanx of beaming church elders and their wives. Everybody said hello and escorted the Alcots inside where Wanda and Delmar made a place for them in the pew. Across the aisle Mildred nodded approvingly. Lester kept staring straight ahead as if he had better things to do.

Chet leaned to his right and whispered in Maureen's ear.

"There's so much brotherly love in here I can't stand it."

That got him a jab in the ribs.

Chet scanned the congregation of righteous faces and leaned to his left.

"I don't see Sheriff Hobbs," he said to Delmar.

"You never will," Delmar said. "The Sheriff doesn't come to service. He says he's the law and the law don't have to."

Chet leaned to Maureen again.

"What's good for the Sheriff," he whispered, "is good enough for me. Pick me up at the local tavern."

He started to get up but Maureen held him down by the sleeve.

"You're staying," she said with a gracious smile that masked a steely voice. "I don't want these people to think I married a heathen. Besides, towns like this keep their taverns closed on Sunday."

Chet heaved a sigh and resigned himself to staying. He submitted to the service, and to the singing, and even to the endless sermonizing. He even put on a sappy smile when they were going out and congratulated Reverend Hipwood on his brevity. That got him another jab in the ribs.

Mrs. Hipwood stepped forward and grasped Maureen's hand. Maureen clutched at Chet's arm as if something sinister was going to happen.

"The ladies of the Rebecca Circle have graciously asked me to invite you to tea this afternoon," Mrs. Hipwood said with a sweet smile. "We're in charge of Christmas decorations and your talents as an artist would be greatly appreciated."

Chet patted Maureen's hand for comfort.

"I'd be delighted," was all Maureen could say.

"And of course you'll be enrolling the children in Sunday School," Mrs. Hipwood added.

"What's Sunday School?" Terry asked.

Maureen jerked his arm to be quiet.

"Of course we will," Maureen said. "As soon as we get organized."

"No better time than now," she said and directed

them to the Fellowship Hall. "The Lord and my husband's work always comes first."

They enrolled the kids in Sunday School and left them standing in front of the hall where the other children were gathering.

Chet looked back as they drove away.

"I feel as though we've betrayed those kids," he said. "They look like abandoned orphans."

"Being invited into the Rebecca Circle on our first visit is a real compliment," Maureen said. "It means we've been accepted."

"I hope you survive the compliment. And I hope the kids survive Sunday School."

"I hope Sunday School survives them," Maureen said.

❄ ❄ ❄

14

December arrived and gray clouds swirled overhead. Occasionally a chill wind blew across the lake and formed a thin shelf of ice around the rim on which ducks gathered. But the moisture-laden lows rolled up from the gulf eight hundred miles to the south, and their warm winds melted the ice. Fog enshrouded the lake each morning, and a thin rain drizzled out of the sky. If snow was falling, it was falling somewhere else.

The school bus roared into the yard and honked its horn. Its doors flew open and twenty kids swarmed out. Maureen and her kids came out of the house and stood on the porch.

"Name's Nannie Moss Hobbs," the lady driver called out and jumped down to the ground. "Kids are anxious to see the haunted house so I gave them two minutes. But don't feel obliged to let them inside."

"Don't worry," Maureen said. "Besides, there are no ghosts inside." When she said it she squeezed

71

each of the twins hands.

Nannie Moss took a little notebook out of her pocket and opened it.

"Fee for taking the kids to school is ten cents per kid," she said. "Or three for a quarter since we're only making one stop. That comes to a dollar and a quarter a week for forty weeks or fifty dollars a year. Any questions?"

"No," Maureen said. "Except I thought school taxes paid for school buses."

"We don't have school taxes," Nannie Moss said. "School's paid for. So are the school buses. Heat and caretaking comes out of the public safety budget because the police and fire department are in the same building. Your bus fee pays for gas, repairs and my salary. Any more questions?"

"No," Maureen said and she couldn't help grinning. "When do I pay?"

"Whenever," Nannie Moss said. "By the week, the month or the year."

She climbed back into the bus and honked the horn twice. The kids scrambled on board and Terry and the twins joined them. The bus's air brakes hissed off and it growled into a sweeping turn.

Maureen expected the kids' faces to be pressed against the windows so she waved. But the kids were already absorbed in talking to their new friends— probably about the ghost that resides inside.

Maureen came down off the porch and looked

across the lake to the old Chippewa burial ground with its fallen dog houses and obliterated markers. Then she looked back at the big white house. It was almost as if she expected some mystical connection to materialize—a spiritual rainbow that spanned their space and time and unified them. But she saw nothing. She couldn't even imagine what it might be. These were two worlds that had clashed at the wrong time in history and would never have the opportunity to touch each other again.

15

The first week of December passed into the second without precipitation. It was as if the clouds had been wrung dry. The only thing that fell out of the sky was Wanda and Delmar, or Lester and Mildred. They always came in pairs and always seemed to know when something needed fixing, which was all the time.

Wanda's pecan pie finally showed up and it was everything Mildred was afraid it was going to be. It would have eclipsed Mildred's cherry pie except Mildred doubled back with an even grander apple pie.

"I'll never learn to bake like this," Maureen said to Chet as she set out a second piece for him and another for herself.

"Don't have to," Chet said between bites. "Just keep the competition going."

Maureen thought about that. She picked up a pencil and started to doodle on her sketch pad. She drew the van with its psychedelic scene. Then she carefully lettered something across it.

"What sounds better?" she asked without looking up. "Mrs. Hobbs Famous Pies? Or Mrs. Hobbs Perfect Pies?"

Chet looked over at what she was doing.

"Going into the pie business?" he asked.

"Just having fun."

"Why not combine the two? *Mrs. Hobbs' Famous Pies. They're perfect.*"

"Not bad," Maureen said. "You should have gone into the advertising business."

"Anything but what I did go into," Chet said.

He picked up the calendar and counted off the days until Christmas.

"According to this there's plenty of time for snow. Winter doesn't even start until the twenty-first of December at 9:43 a.m., Eastern Standard Time, or 2:43 p.m., Greenwich Mean Time."

"What does the Happy Weatherman say?" Maureen asked.

Chet leaned over and turned on the television set. After three interminable commercials, the Happy Weatherman bounced onto the screen.

"Michigan's Upper Peninsula is experiencing record snowfall," the Happy Weatherman said. "Skiing in Marquette, Houghton and Ontonagon is the best in years."

"Hear that?" Chet said. "Maybe we'll get some too."

"As for down here," the announcer continued, "the Happy Weatherman bodes no hope for a white Christmas. Another low moving up from the Gulf of Mexico is keeping the cold Canadian weather at bay. If anything comes our way it'll be rain but even that's unlikely. Only the powerful jet stream can put an end to the drought afflicting this part of the state, and the jet stream hasn't moved in a month."

Chet turned down the volume and looked at Maureen.

"How do you move a jet stream?" he asked.

"If the mountain won't come to Mohammed," she said, "maybe we should take Mohammed to the mountain."

"You've got that backwards."

"No I don't. We've got to do something for Terry. We can't just sit here."

"What do you propose we do? Pray for snow?"

"I've already tried that. Maybe we should drive up to the real Ontonagon and spend Christmas in a motel."

"Sounds delightful," Chet said without enthusiasm. "But you heard what the weatherman said. Skiing's the best in years. We wouldn't even be able to rent a stable."

"Very appropriate for this time of year," Maureen said.

"Right, and the twins could sleep in the manger. We'll just have to stay here and hope for the best."

Chet went to the window and looked up at the gray clouds roiling the sky above the lake.

"It's all right there," he said, his voice almost prayerful. "Just waiting to come down. All it needs is somebody or something to pull the chain and whump!—dump the whole load in our laps."

Maureen came up and stood by his side.

"You know what that's called?" Maureen said.

"No," Chet said. "Is there a technical term for it?"

"Yes. It's called a miracle."

16

Chet, Maureen and the kids trudged across country for what seemed like five miles without finding what they were looking for.

"This will be great for cross country skiing," Maureen said.

"Right," Chet said. "All we need is—"

"Snow!" they all shouted in unison.

Chet went up to a stunted evergreen, took hold of its misshapen trunk and tried to straighten it.

"Think this'll pass for a *Tannenbaum*?" he asked.

"What's a *Tannenbaum*?" Terry asked.

"German for Christmas tree. From whence came our tradition. Although this specimen looks a mite too disreputable to be a real *Tannenbaum*."

Maureen stepped back for the long shot.

"I'm afraid you're right," she said. "It looks awfully scrawny."

"I like the way it smells," Jennifer said and buried her face in the boughs. "Like Pine-Sol."

"I like it too," Suzy said. "It's the nicest we've seen."

Maureen looked hopefully at Chet. "We haven't seen many others."

"Can I cut it down?" Terry said, eager to perform surgery.

"I don't know," Maureen said. "This land isn't ours."

Chet looked around. "I don't see anybody telling us not to."

"That's not the point," Maureen said. "This tree probably belongs to the Chippewas."

"Please," Chet said. "I feel bad enough about the wood we've been burning." He passed the saw to Terry. "The Chippewas are forty miles away and this is for a good cause."

Terry sawed through the little trunk in a twinkle. Then they dragged the tree home and set it up in the parlor.

"It looks pretty sad," Chet said. "Maybe we should have let it grow for a few more years."

"It'll be fine," Maureen said.

Chet leaned close to her and said quietly, "Shouldn't it be more than just fine? Especially this year?"

Maureen squeezed his arm.

"Don't worry, hon. By the time we get through with it, it'll look wonderful."

She opened her box of ornaments.

"Oops!" she said. "Foiled from the start. There aren't as many decorations here as I thought there were."

"We meant to buy some, remember?" Chet said. "I guess Christmas got lost in the move."

"We can still buy some," Maureen said. "If the budget can stand it."

"Why don't we decorate it with popcorn?" Jennifer said. "That's what we're using at school."

"Popcorn!" Terry said with disdain. "That'll look weird."

"Popcorn will be great," Chet said nudging Terry. "Especially if we butter it, and mom makes us some punch."

The kids jumped up and down and cheered.

"How about a wassail bowl?" Maureen said. "We can give it a test-run for Christmas."

"Don't you mean a taste-run?" Chet said.

Maureen went into the kitchen while Chet took the popper down from its hook next to the fireplace. He dusted and oiled it, and layered the bottom with corn. Then he passed the popper to Terry.

Terry jiggled the popper over the fire until the exploding kernels banged furiously against the copper lid. When the lid rose and the exploding ceased, Terry dumped the freshly popped corn into a bowl. Suzy stirred in the melted butter and they dug their fingers into it like starving waifs.

"It's going to take forever to fill this bowl," Chet said. "We're eating it faster than we're making it."

Maureen brought in the steaming wassail bowl and everybody gathered around for a toast.

"To Christmas," Chet said raising his brimming cup. "I think this is going to be the most wonderful Christmas ever!"

"To Christmas!" they all said and drank.

Maureen immediately confiscated the unbuttered popcorn and she and the twins started threading the garland. Chet dug into the box and drew out the single string of lights. He counted the bulbs one by one.

"Only thirty six," he said. "It's going to take a lot of ingenuity to make these look like more than they are."

"Like the loaves and fishes?" Jennifer said.

"Only I'm no miracle worker," Chet said. He leaned over to Maureen. "See what they learn at Sunday School?"

Chet and Terry wove the single string of lights skillfully through the tree so every bulb would be visible from every angle. To make sure, they plugged in the string and turned off the lights.

"Not bad," Chet said, pleased at the effect. "We may have unraveled the mystery of the loaves and fishes."

"Don't blaspheme," Maureen warned. "It could get you into a lot of trouble."

She climbed up on a chair and tied the end of the garland to the tip of the tree. The twins fed her the rest in a continuous rope which she draped around the tree in a looping spiral. The twins then attached the few ornaments to the bare branches and they all stepped back to admire their handiwork.

Maureen pursed her lips. "I wish—" she started to say.

"I wish we had more of these old-fashioned ornaments," Suzy said. "They look like giant snowflakes."

"These are all we'll ever have, honey," Maureen said, fingering one of the delicately crocheted stars. "Your grandmother made them a long time ago."

"Why don't we make some out of paper?" Jennifer said.

"Yes!" Suzy said. "We could cut out tons, and cover the tree like real snow!"

"With paper?" Terry said sourly.

"It might look very interesting," Maureen said. "Let's try it. If we don't like it, we can always take them down."

The twins got out a stack of note pads and folded the small sheets into squares and then into triangles. They used their tiny snub-nosed scissors to cut random patterns into the triangles. Unfolded, the triangles became intricate snowflakes about the size of a teacup.

Chet got out the iron and pressed the snowflakes flat. Then Terry sprayed them with starch and passed them to Maureen who hung them from every bough. The scrawny little pine was being transformed into a Christmas tree unlike any they had ever seen before.

Chet turned off the lights. The effect was dazzling. The little tree seemed to have grown into a majestic *Tannenbaum* that literally sparkled in the dark.

"Wow!" said Terry, his eyes opened wide. "It's gorgeous!"

Chet started to sing, as much to his own surprise as to the others'. He sang quietly at first, but as he found his voice his words rang loud and clear.

"Oh Tannenbaum, Oh Tannenbaum,
Thy leaves are so unchanging.
Oh Christmas Tree, Oh Christmas Tree,
Thy leaves are so unchanging.
Not only green when summer's here,
But also when it's cold and drear.
Oh Tannenbaum, Oh Christmas Tree!
Thy leaves are so unchanging!"

When Chet finished Maureen burst into applause. The kids joined in with the applause and Terry whistled loudly.

"I didn't know you could sing," Maureen said to Chet.

"Neither did I," Chet said. "The tree must have inspired me."

"That poor, disreputable thing we dragged in from the cold?"

"Maybe there's a lesson here for all of us. This humble little tree is helping us remember the real meaning of Christmas. There's a lot more to it than flashing lights and electronic games."

"What *is* the real meaning of Christmas?" Jennifer asked.

Maureen leaned back in her chair and looked at Chet with a mischievous grin.

"Yes dear," she said ingenuously. "We'd love to hear what you have to say on the subject. Wouldn't we, kids?"

The kids cheered and sat down in a circle in front of the tree. Chet knew he was being sandbagged but conceded gracefully and sat down with them. He cleared his throat even though it didn't need clearing.

"The real meaning of Christmas," Chet said. "Now let me see—where shall I begin?"

"Why, at the beginning," Maureen said.

❄ ❄ ❄

17

"Christmas is really a pagan holiday," Chet said.

Maureen was aghast. "That isn't true!"

"Yes it is," Chet said. "The druids in ancient England chose that day as a day of celebration. Does anybody know why?"

"The days were starting to get longer!" Terry replied.

"That's right. So when the Christians decided to celebrate Jesus' birthday they chose the same day."

"Why are you telling them this?" Maureen said. "You know they repeat everything at school."

"But it's true," Terry said. "I learned about the druids in school."

"Not in a Mittenville school, you didn't," Maureen said.

"Does that mean Jesus wasn't born on Christmas day?" Suzy asked.

"Nobody knows for sure when he was born," Chet said. "Some people think it was in October."

"Now you've done it," Maureen said.

"The Bible knows," Jennifer said. "Luke says there were shepherds abiding in the fields, keeping watch over their flocks by night. And they were sore afraid when the angel of the Lord came down to tell them about it."

"That's very good," Chet said. "But those shepherds were so sore afraid they forgot to write it down. Now nobody knows what really happened. Let that be a lesson to you. Write everything important down."

"I always do," Suzy said. "I wrote about the ghost in my diary."

"We all know Jesus was born," Chet continued. "Everybody's pretty sure of that. Probably in a stable because there was no room in the inn."

"Didn't they know Mary was pregnant?" Jennifer asked.

Chet shot a glance at Maureen. "When did they learn about that?"

Maureen just shrugged.

"The inn must have been crowded with big shooters," Chet said. "Like it would be today. So all the rooms would have been taken. And Jesus' folks were poor so they couldn't buy their way in. Carpenters didn't make a lot of money in those days."

"Like Lester," Suzy said. "Only Joseph didn't have a van to carry his family and tools. All he had was a donkey."

"Could one donkey carry all that stuff?" Terry asked.

"We try not to sweat the details," Chet said. "Luke's interpretation is very imaginative. That's why we like it so much."

A pained look crossed Suzy's face. "You mean the Book of Luke isn't true?"

"It's not exactly not true," Chet said. "The facts of Christmas may be fuzzy but the truth is well understood. All Luke did was try to tell the story in a way people would remember. I think he did a pretty good job, don't you?"

"Was Jesus born in a manger or wasn't he?" Suzy persisted.

"I'd say it was very likely," Chet said. "It's as good a place as any, and more imaginative than most."

"And did the three wise men bring gifts of gold, frankincense and myrrh?" Jennifer asked.

"That's pretty exact," Terry said. "Sounds like somebody wrote that down."

"Could be," Chet said. "But as I said, details aren't important. What is important is what Jesus taught when he grew up."

"I know what he taught," Terry said. "Love thy neighbor, and turn the other cheek when somebody slugs you."

"That's about right," Chet said.

"How come we don't do it?" Jennifer asked.

"Nobody does it," Terry said. "You'd be a sucker

if you did."

"Actually, we do it all the time," Chet said. "You know how grouchy everybody gets at this time of year? People don't like driving home in the dark. It gets slushy outside and your feet get wet. Or your windshield wipers clog just when traffic starts to get heavy because everybody's running around at the last minute buying presents they don't really want to buy. Pretty soon people start cussing one another out."

"Honking their horns too," Terry said. "I saw you do it."

"I'm afraid you did," Chet said. "But on Christmas Eve a curious thing happens. Everything sort of slows right down and all the hysteria evaporates. Tree lights come on and candles are lighted. Before you know it, the same people who were cussing are now going from house to house singing about love and joy and goodwill to men. And everybody is saying 'Merry Christmas' to everybody else, even to complete strangers."

"That's good," Suzy said, "because you never know who the stranger might be."

"Very good, dear," Maureen said and patted her on the shoulder.

"In fact," Chet went on, "the goodness of Christmas is so powerful, it wipes away the badness of the entire day or the entire year. Sometimes it even wipes away the badness of a lifetime the way it did with old Mr. Scrooge."

"I never thought of Christmas that way," Terry said.

"But all that goodness didn't just happen," Chet said. "It came about because a long time ago in Bethlehem, a little kid was born."

Maureen started to sing—

"Away in a manger, no crib for His bed,
The little Lord Jesus lay down His sweet head."

The children added their own delicate voices to hers.

"The stars in the heavens looked down where He lay,
The little Lord Jesus asleep on the hay."

Chet joined in and together they sang—

"The cattle are lowing, the baby awakes,
But little Lord Jesus no crying He makes.
I love thee, Lord Jesus look down from the sky
And stay by my cradle till morning is nigh."

Maureen leaned over and kissed Chet on the cheek.

"Not a bad recovery," she said. "Quite inspirational, too."

"Thanks," Chet said proudly. "I thought it was pretty good myself." He got to his feet. "And now I'd like to propose a toast to the tree that's inspiring us all." He raised his cup and faced the tree. "To the finest tree we've ever had. Merry Christmas, Mr. Tannenbaum!"

They all drank. Then everybody started to sing—

89

"We wish you a Merry Christmas!
We wish you a Merry Christmas!
We wish you a Merry Christmas
And a Happy New Year!"

At the conclusion of the song Suzy held up her cup and said, "Merry Christmas, Mr. Ghost!"

Everybody looked in the direction Suzy was looking but nothing was there. Suddenly everybody burst out laughing. With or without the snow, it was going to be a wonderful Christmas!

❄ ❄ ❄

18

Maureen studied the noisy decorating on the side of the van, this time with an artist's critical eye. Before, it was just a van trying to attract attention. Now it was a marketing vehicle. Everything on it would have to communicate precisely. Nothing more, nothing less. Even the psychedelic paint scheme would have to make marketing sense.

She carefully masked off an area on each side of the van and used an air brush to stencil in three rows of lettering.

> *Mrs. Hobbs Famous Pies*
> *They're Perfect!*
> *Homemade in Mittenville, Michigan*

When she finished she went up on the porch to get a customer's eye-view. She concluded she liked the way the van looked. In fact she liked it so much she called Chet out to get his critique.

Chet squinted at the van from several angles, made a sour face and rested his chin in his hand.

"The words are getting lost in the graphics," he said. "I wish you had let me paint it over."

"You're over-thinking it," Maureen said. "Just react, okay? Like it, don't like it. Which one is it?"

"Let's just say I wouldn't have done it that way," Chet said. "Is anybody going to know what you're selling?"

Maureen sighed heavily.

"At least they'll know it's something different!" She stomped off the porch and climbed into the van. "I'm off to see how it works."

"Wait a minute," Chet said. "You can't go like that. You left off the apostrophe."

Maureen looked at him as if he had lost it.

"Left off the what?"

"The apostrophe. In Mrs. Hobbs' Famous Pies. An apostrophe signifies that Mrs. Hobbs is possessive. Grammatically speaking."

"Mrs. Hobbs is not possessive," Maureen said. "She's an adjective. As in apple pie. We don't say apple's pie, do we?"

"No," Chet said, "but this is different. Mrs. Hobbs should have an apostrophe because they're her pies."

Maureen studied him for a protracted moment.

"That's just it," she said. "I don't want to give people the impression that Mrs. Hobbs owns the pies. Only that she made them."

She blew Chet an air kiss and took off.

"Okay," Chet said as he watched the van bounce

93

merrily up the rutted road. "It's your funeral."

Maureen collected six apple and six cherry pies from Mrs. Mildred Hobbs and carefully stacked them inside the van. She picked up six pecan and six mincemeat pies from Mrs. Wanda Hobbs and segregated them, as promised, on the other side of the van. Then she headed for the highway and Dearborn.

She barely got to Midland when a police car flashed its lights and the officer waved her over. Maureen pulled into a supermarket parking lot and stopped. The police car drew up alongside and two officers got out.

Not an auspicious beginning, Maureen said to herself. When the cops walked up, she rolled down the window and put on her best what-did-I-do-officer? expression.

"What did I do, officer?" she said as pitifully as she could without sounding too corny.

"What kind of pies are you selling?" the officer asked.

"All kinds," Maureen said, momentarily flustered. "Why? Do I need some kind of license? I'm only passing through."

"I wouldn't know about that," the officer said. "I'd just like to buy one if they're really homemade."

"Homemade?" Maureen brightened. "Let me show you just how homemade they really are!"

She got out of the van, opened the rear doors and

took out one of Mildred's colossal apple pies.

"You're a lucky man if your wife can make an apple pie like this."

"My wife makes lousy pies," the first cop said. "I'll take two."

"So will I," the second cop said. "And I'm not even married."

"They're expensive," Maureen said. "Twelve dollars apiece."

"For a pie like that?" the first officer said. "It's cheap."

Maureen sold them each a cherry and an apple pie and they drove off with a genial "Merry Christmas!" She was about to close the doors on the van when a man came up.

"Are you selling those pies here?" he asked.

"I guess I am," Maureen said. "Would you like to buy one? They're fabulous."

"I can see that," the man said. "No, I'm not interested in buying one. This is my parking lot, and that's my food store over there."

"Ohh!" Maureen groaned. "I'm sorry. I guess I'm guilty of practising unfair competition right on your own property."

"Unfair to say the least," the man said peering inside the van. "I have never seen pies like that. I'd like to buy the whole load. Unless of course they're already spoken for."

"No they're not," Maureen said, delighted. "You

can have them all. I was going to sell them door-to-door to my old friends in Dearborn."

"I wouldn't want your friends to be disappointed."

"They won't be," Maureen said. "They didn't know I was coming."

"Then why don't we make it short and sweet? From your van to my store?"

"They're expensive," Maureen said. "Twice what a pie-store charges."

"Premium wares should be expensive," the man said and held out his hand to be shaken.

"Deal!" Maureen said and shook it.

"Great. How many more pies can you deliver before Christmas?"

19

Chet watched Maureen sort the money and stack it in neat piles on the kitchen table.

"Imagine," she said breathlessly. "A contract to deliver as many pies as we can make. And on our first day. Maybe our luck has turned."

"That's wonderful," Chet said. "But how many pies can two ladies make?"

"We're looking into leasing the old pizza store on Main Street," Maureen said. "The ovens are still there, and Wanda and Mildred think they may be able to retrain the laid-off workers."

"What about a license?"

"For what?"

"Possession with intent to sell pies. You know how the Sheriff is."

Maureen dismissed his concerns with a wave.

"I'll worry about that when we get this sucker up and running. Right now I'm more interested in counting greenbacks!"

Chet went into the foyer and got his coat.

"Where are you going?" Maureen asked.

"Into town to inquire about a license. I have to go to the hardware store anyway."

"You're too meticulous for your own good," she said and followed him to the front door. "Nobody cares about a license."

"I'll bet the Sheriff does." Chet kissed her on the cheek. "I just hope nobody notices."

"What?"

"That I'm driving a vehicle without apostrophes."

Chet climbed into the van which now smelled delicious and took off up the rutted road to Mittenville. He couldn't understand why Maureen was always so reluctant to inquire about anything she was ignorant of, like licenses. Refusing to inquire or ask for directions was usually the male role. In this case their roles were decidedly reversed.

It probably had something to do with her artistic temperament, he decided. She's right-brain creative, he's left-brain logical. Not a compatible combination to begin with. Throw in some female hormones and the difference becomes acute. Like the debate over apostrophes.

Chet parked the van carefully and inconspicuously so it would not incur the wrath of either the law or Dirty Harry. He shook his head when he realized how intimidated he was. Not a bad psychology for a Sheriff, he thought. And the perfect environment for a police state.

He went into the Department of Public Safety and pushed through the glass doors into the Sheriff's offices. Delmar was sitting with his feet up on the desk, watching television.

"Morning, Delmar," Chet said. "Is Dirty Harry in?"

"He's taking a nap in the Sheriff's office," Delmar said without looking up.

"Then I can relax," Chet said. "What's on the tube?"

"*The Simpsons*," Delmar said. "Pretty hilarious stuff."

The door to the Sheriff's office opened and Dirty Harry trotted out. He emitted a guttural snarl and walked stiffly up to Chet. Chet went rigid as the dog started sniffing him in all the wrong places. Sheriff Hobbs appeared in the doorway and suspiciously eyed Chet.

"Pies," Chet said uneasily. "Harry probably likes the smell."

"What are you putting in them?" the Sheriff asked.

"Wanda and Mildred make the pies," Delmar said dryly.

The Sheriff looked to see what Delmar was watching.

"That VCR is government property," he said. "You know better than to play civilian tapes on it."

"I've already seen *America's Most Wanted* three times," Delmar grumbled. "I know the names and

99

faces of every fugitive by heart."

"Then put on *Top Cops* or *NYPD Blue*. Law enforcement officers can't see that stuff often enough."

Delmar dropped his feet off the desk and ejected the tape. He fished another out of the desk and shoved it into the VCR.

The Sheriff squinted at Chet. "What are you in here for, Alcot?"

"Not to be violated by a dog."

The Sheriff snapped his fingers and Dirty Harry slinked under the desk and sat down.

"I'm here because I'd like to know if my wife needs a license for her pie business," Chet said. "To keep everything pristine, as you would say."

"Don't know if she needs a license," the Sheriff said. "Nobody in this town ever trafficked in pies before. We had a mill and a wiredrawing plant. Even a bakery once. But no dessert factory. Have to talk to the Town Council about that. We'll be sure to let you know. Anything else on your mind?"

"That was it," Chet said.

"Another thing this town never had," the Sheriff said, "is a newspaper. You used to be in publishing, Alcot. Ain't publishing like journalism?"

"Nothing like it," Chet said.

"Nothing?" The Sheriff was skeptical. "You put words down on paper, don't you? And move them around to alter the meaning?"

"I never looked at it that way," Chet said.

"Why couldn't you start a newspaper?"

"Why would I want to?"

"Didn't say you'd want to," the Sheriff said. "It's the town that wants it. And they wouldn't much care who ran it."

"Is that right," Chet said coolly. "Well it's a big investment in money and time. I don't think I can spare either."

"Not having money to spare I can understand," the Sheriff said. "But I'm curious as to why you might not have the time. You were laid off from your last job, weren't you?"

Chet felt his ire rise.

"You've been checking on me again, haven't you?"

"Routine," the Sheriff said. "No harm meant."

"You're causing a lot of harm, Sheriff. The Supreme Court recognized privacy as a right guaranteed by the Constitution. You are flagrantly violating that right."

The Sheriff assumed his swaggering pose.

"Nobody accuses me of violating the Constitution," he said sternly. "I took an oath to protect it. Whatever is on the public record is open to the public, and every citizen has a right to access it."

Chet stared at him in cold fury. He was going to say something but thought better of it. Instead he turned on his heel and stalked out.

Delmar looked up from the television.

"For someone who ain't a lawyer," he said, "that fella sure knows a lot about the Supreme Court."

"Maybe," the Sheriff said. "But I know a lot about this county. And this county is the only supreme court that counts."

❋ ❋ ❋

20

Reverend Wilbur Hipwood leaned against the lectern and waited for the elders and their wives to settle down and stop scraping their wooden chairs across the floor. They were worse than the kids.

"Are we all here?" he said over the din.

"Elder Slocum isn't," Elder Forbush said.

"Can't spend our lives waitin' on Sam," Elder Mudge said. "Let's get on with it."

The Reverend consulted his watch.

"We have a grave duty to perform," he said. "The sooner we do it the better. Shall we proceed?"

He waited until he had the rapt silence of the pious and resumed speaking with a practiced quaver in his voice.

"We are gathered here in Fellowship Hall in extraordinary session," he said. "The Apples of Sodom have fallen into our midst. Outwardly pleasing to the eye, they are rotten at the core and will inevitably corrupt all those with whom they come in contact."

An uneasy murmur emanated from the group.

"Our children are our future," the Reverend went on. "It is their future that is at risk. It is our duty to protect them—from drugs, sex and violence; from diseases of the body and soul; from the Apples of Sodom. We must root out the threat where we find it, and cast it out of the community. My dear wife Flossie will now present us with a bill of particulars that clearly defines the ominous threat posed by the Alcot family to our community."

Reverend Hipwood sat down and Mrs. Hipwood took his place at the lectern. She inhaled deeply. This would be her first opportunity to demonstrate to her husband and the council how effective she could be, and she desperately wanted to be eloquent.

"Item one," she said clearly and resolutely. "It is their testament that Christmas is really a pagan holiday."

The group muttered softly among themselves.

"Item two," Flossie said over the muttering. "It is their testament that Jesus Christ was not born on Christmas day, and that the Book of Luke is a work of the *imagination*."

The muttering grew louder.

"Who are we talking about?" Elder Slocum said coming in through the back door. "Shouldn't we get that on the record?"

Flossie became momentarily flustered and looked

feebly at her husband. The Reverend sprang to his feet.

"Everybody who was here on time knows we're talking about the Alcot family," the Reverend said patiently. "That is already on the record."

"You mean the new couple that moved in out Lake Ontonagon way?"

"That's right."

"Who are they giving all these testaments to?"

"That most impressionable body of all," the Reverend said. "Their own children. And their children are transporting this heresy to Sunday school and contaminating our children, and your grandchildren. Now may we please continue, Elder Slocum?"

"Just wanted to get it clarified," Slocum said and sat down.

"Item three!" Flossie said with heightened volume but considerably less confidence. "It is their testament that the existence of the Three Wise Men is unimportant!"

She closed her eyes the way she had rehearsed and shook her head woefully.

"Item four: It is their testament that our yuletide traditions come from Germany where the Christmas tree originated!"

"I think it did," Slocum said.

"You're missing the point," the Reverend said with forbearance. "We are not quibbling over content here, but intent. The Alcots' intent is clearly heretical, and unmistakably atheistic."

He motioned for Flossie to continue.

"Item five," Flossie said lowering her voice for dramatic effect and raising it with each succeeding phrase. "It is their testament that God kills living things; that God makes mistakes; and that everybody gets ornery at this time of the year!"

"There's a lot of truth to that last statement," Slocum said and got a modest chuckle from some in the group.

"Item six!" Flossie said ignoring the interruption. "It is their testament that they have duplicated the miracle of the loaves and the fishes!"

Flossie peered over her glasses at her fascinated audience. She was feeling in control for the first time.

"In conclusion," she said with a tremor, "Mr. Alcot has regretfully stated before his own children that he does not know what he believes in. I'll repeat that. *He said he does not know what he believes in!*"

The muttering grew very loud.

"That, ladies and gentlemen, is the bill of particulars," Flossie said. "I would now like to turn the meeting over to Reverend Hipwood."

The Reverend returned to the lectern and gave Flossie a discreet squeeze of the hand that told her she had performed splendidly. She returned to her seat, triumphant in her cause.

"The challenge is laid before us," Reverend Hipwood said solemnly. "Do we close our eyes to the Devil in our midst? Or do we take our lead from Holy Scripture and cast the Satan out? I remind you that it is our children who are at risk here—the most precious commodity we have."

The conversation grew loud again. Elder Forbush stood up and waited for silence. When he didn't get it he decided to speak anyway.

"These particulars are not what worries me, Reverend!" he shouted over the hubbub. "What worries me, and should worry all of you, is that the Alcot family's got AIDS!"

❅ ❅ ❅

21

F orbush knew from the stunned reaction of the elders and their wives that he had dropped a bombshell.

"Who told you they've got AIDS?" Slocum said.

"Everybody knows that," Mrs. Mudge said.

"Is that true?" Elder Denby said.

"I didn't know that," Mrs. Buxton said.

"Why are we wasting time with the Three Wise Men?" Mudge said. "We should be dealing with the real issue!"

Reverend Hipwood quieted them by raising his hands.

"That was next on our agenda," he said. "Thank you for bringing it forward, Elder Forbush. Indeed, it has come to our attention that the Alcot family has fallen victim to that sinful disease. A disease that is always fatal because it disables the body's immune system. Of special importance to us and our children is the fact that AIDS can be transmitted in very common ways. Ways that expose our children to its contamination."

"What ways?" Slocum asked.

"I am not a physician," Reverend Hipwood said. "But current wisdom says a pinprick is all that's needed to communicate this calumny."

"That means we're all in danger!" Mrs. Buxton said.

"AIDS is a curse of God!" Denby shouted. "It smites the wicked and the children of the wicked!"

"It is not our place to sit in judgment," the Reverend said.

"Their testaments brought this curse down upon their heads!" Mrs. Denby said. "Do we want them spreading it to our families?"

"We do not!" the Reverend said loudly as he tried to keep control of the meeting. "We can't allow this disease to spread through our midst any more than we can allow the propagation of heresy and atheism. It is not our place to judge, but it is our sacred duty to protect. After much soul-searching and consultation with some of you and with God—"

"I'd be interested to hear what God had to say on the subject," Slocum said.

The Reverend ignored the remark.

"I'd like to propose drastic but humane action to save our church, our schools, and our community," the Reverend went on. He lifted his eyes heavenward. "It is with a heavy but a charitable heart that I propose this unfortunate family be quarantined until such time as they are cured, spiritually and physically."

"Why didn't you say so in the first place?" Mudge said. "We could have saved a lot of time."

"Just a minute!" Slocum said indignantly. "You said AIDS is incurable. A quarantine is the same as banishing them forever!"

"Not if we put our faith in Christ," the Reverend said. "He has cured the halt and the lame, and brought the dead back to life."

"You're condemning that family to permanent exile," Slocum said. "For all we know they're innocent victims."

"God does not spare the innocent," Mrs. Denby said. "Why should we?"

"How can we go against God's will?" Elder Buxton said.

"How do you know what God's will is?" Slocum asked.

"Get on with it," Mudge said. "I second the motion to quarantine."

"We have a motion on the floor," Reverend Hipwood said. "Is there any discussion?"

"We've had our discussion," Mudge said. "Let's vote."

"What's the big hurry?" Slocum said. "On your way to a poker game?"

"Velta and I have to drive to Traverse City, if you don't mind!"

"Traverse City can wait," Slocum said. "We're talking about people's lives here. We have neither the moral nor the legal authority to place them under quarantine."

"Let's not get hysterical," Buxton said. "We're within our rights. We used to quarantine families for scarlet fever all the time."

"I'm not hysterical and it isn't the same," Slocum said.

"I see no difference," Buxton said.

"Quarantine is a merciful compromise," Reverend Hipwood said. "It protects the community without treating the offenders like lepers."

"But it does treat them like lepers," Slocum said. "In a most cruel and unChristian way."

"Aw, shut up, Slocum," Buxton said. "What do you know about Christian ways? You're never here anyway."

"Can't we get on with this?" Mudge said. "I haven't got all day."

"You people are pretty cavalier with this family's future," Slocum said. "I wonder if you'd be that callous with your own?"

"Don't worry," Mudge sneered. "My family would never get into a fix like this."

"Let's knock off the kibitzing and vote," Buxton said. "I have other fish to fry too."

"May we have a show of hands?" the Reverend said. "Those in favor of the motion to quarantine—

elders only, please."

Nearly every elder's hand went up.

"Opposed?"

Only Elder Slocum raised his hand in opposition.

"The motion carries," Reverend Hipwood said. "I assume, since the Town Council is represented here, the motion has civil weight?"

There was a general murmur of approval.

"Can we make it unanimous?" Reverend Hipwood said looking directly at Elder Slocum. "It would lend the resolution greater moral force."

"This resolution has no moral force," Slocum said as he got up and headed for the door. "You want to make it unanimous? I'll make it unanimous for you. You are all asses, every last one of you, and I refuse to have anything to do with you or your resolution. And let that be my formal notice of resignation."

"Don't do anything you'll be sorry for in the morning," the Reverend said. "We need to stick together on this."

"Let him go!" Mudge snapped. "He's always been a contrarian anyway."

"Good riddance!" Buxton muttered but still loud enough to be heard.

Slocum tugged on his coat.

"While I'm at it," he said, "I resign from the Town Council too."

"He'll be back," Forbush said. "With his tail between his legs."

"I don't think we want him back," Buxton said.

"If I do come back," Slocum said, "it'll be only after you idiots come to your senses. And that may be never." He paused before going out. "I'm ashamed of you. Every single one of you."

Slocum brushed past Wanda Hobbs on the way out. She was not the wife of an elder and was watching the proceedings from the hall. Even though nobody else knew she was there, and Slocum barely noticed her, she felt compelled to hang her head in shame.

22

"There's a cruel way to do this, and a humane way," Reverend Hipwood confided to Sheriff Hobbs. "This is the cruel way."

The Sheriff stared distastefully at the paper the Reverend was holding. He reached for it but the Reverend withdrew it. Sheriff Hobbs smelled a rat and leaned back in his chair.

"A quarantine is cruel, all right," the Sheriff said. "What's the humane way?"

Reverend Hipwood leaned across the desk.

"Cancel the lease," he said in a low voice. "The Alcots will be forced to leave town because nobody else will rent to them. We can accomplish the same purpose without hurting anybody's feelings."

"When?"

"The sooner the better. But not on Christmas Eve."

"Of course not," the Sheriff said. "We want to keep this as humane as possible. Is this your idea?"

The Reverend nodded smugly.

"Kind of ruthless for a man of the cloth, isn't it?"

the Sheriff said.

"On the contrary. It spares their feelings so it's really rather kind. And it removes the risk from our children, which is our primary objective."

Reverend Hipwood suddenly grew intense.

"That is the single most important factor in all of this, Sheriff," he said. "Our children must not be exposed to the AIDS virus! Our whole community could be wiped out if they are!"

"Aren't you being melodramatic, Reverend? Only homos get AIDS."

"Not true," the Reverend said. "Anybody can get it because there are many ways to pass it. Hypodermic needles, blood transfusions, exchange of bodily fluids. So many ways we can't take the chance of exposing our children to any of them. When they come of age they can make their own decisions. While they're children we have to protect them. Will you cancel the lease?"

"Can't do it," the Sheriff said. "They paid six months in advance."

"Give them back all their money. The Town Council has authorized me to cover your losses."

"Those cheapskates? Where were they when we needed a new patrol car?"

"Actually, some of the more active members made personal commitments."

"I said I can't do it," the Sheriff said. "The Alcots are good tenants. I'd have no reason to cancel their lease."

"Find a reason."

The Sheriff shot the Reverend a withering glance.

"I don't do that!" he said.

"You mean you'd rather see them suffer the pain and humiliation of being quarantined?"

"I don't much like that idea either," the Sheriff said. He snapped the paper out of the Reverend's hand and looked at it. "Strictly speaking this is church work. You'll have to take care of it yourself."

"That is an instrument of the Town Council," the Reverend said. "As our chief law enforcement officer, you are required to deliver it. And enforce it."

The Sheriff tilted the paper towards the light.

"So it is," he mumbled quietly. "I should have known."

"You'll reconsider?"

"My hands are tied," the Sheriff said. "As chief law enforcement officer, it is my duty to see that the laws in this county are upheld, not broken."

"Not even bent? For the most charitable of reasons?"

"What's right is right, and what's wrong is wrong," the Sheriff said. "I don't know why you people can't get that through your heads. I'll serve your paper because I'm required to. But don't talk to me about charity. The last place you're supposed to look for it is in a police station. You usually find it in a church."

❋ ❋ ❋

23

"Starting a newspaper isn't such a bad idea," Maureen said to Chet through a mouthful of pins. "I'll bet your editorials would become famous."

She patted Suzy on the tutu and moved her off the stool.

"There, honey. You look exactly like the Littlest Angel."

Now Jennifer took her turn on the stool.

"*I* want to be the Littlest Angel," she said.

"Maybe this year they'll have two," Maureen said. "I'll bet they've never had twin angels before."

"Do you know how much it costs to start a newspaper?" Chet said.

He finished tightening the carved wooden crutch and handed it to Terry. "Try that, tiger."

"It costs less than it used to," Maureen said. "Today you can use computers and desk-top publishing."

"Where would I get the money for a computer?"

"If the town wants a newspaper bad enough

they'll pay for it."

"That'll be the day," Chet said. "Besides, I'm not that eager to put anything into this community. All they've done since we've been here is try to throw us in jail."

"That's not true, dear. They've accepted us very nicely."

Terry hobbled across the library on the crutch.

"It works great, Dad!" he said. "Do I look like Tiny Tim?"

"Best one I've seen."

Chet heard a car approaching and went to the window.

"It's the Sheriff. Wonder what he wants now?"

Maureen groaned.

"He must be coming to tell us about the pie license. You had to go and ask!"

Chet watched Sheriff Hobbs get out of the car and walk up onto the porch.

"Looks like he brought the license with him so he can collect the fee," he said. "These small town hicks don't miss a trick."

The doorbell rang and Chet went to the door and opened it. Sheriff Hobbs was standing there looking at his feet.

"Sorry to bother you, Mr. Alcot," the Sheriff said in an uncharacteristically subdued manner. "But I've got something important to discuss with you."

"About the pie license?" Chet asked.

The Sheriff shook his head. "Haven't had the chance to look into that."

"Then what's on your mind?"

"I'd like to speak to Mrs. Alcot too, if I may."

Chet swung the door open and let the Sheriff in. He led him into the library where Maureen looked up from her pinning.

"Hi, Sheriff," she said. "Kids, say hi to the Sheriff."

"Hi, Sheriff!" the kids said.

The Sheriff nodded his greeting and took off his Mountie hat. It was the first time they had seen him hatless. They couldn't help smirking at his thinning hair.

"I'm in the school play," Terry said. "Guess who this is?"

He hobbled around on his crutch.

"Tiny Tim?" the Sheriff said with difficulty.

"We're the Littlest Angels," Jennifer said.

"The twins are in the nativity scene at church," Maureen said. "They helped me design their costumes."

"Cute," the Sheriff said and awkwardly cleared his throat. "Could we excuse the children, please? I'm here on grown-up business."

"Let's excuse ourselves," Maureen said. "It's easier."

She led Chet and the Sheriff across the foyer into the parlor.

"Can we close these?" the Sheriff asked and drew

the sliding doors together.

"Sure," Chet said and looked curiously at Maureen.

The Sheriff saw the Christmas tree and appeared surprised.

"I didn't expect to see a tree—that nice," he said.

"It took us long enough to find it," Chet said. "What's up?"

"I'm here on a very unpleasant mission," the Sheriff said, putting his hat under his arm adopting an official pose. "It is my duty to inform you that as of now this house is quarantined."

"Quarantined?" Maureen said. "What on earth for?"

"AIDS."

Maureen's shoulders slumped and she looked at Chet.

"So that's your grown-up business," Chet said. "Nobody gets quarantined for AIDS. I've never heard of that."

The Sheriff unfolded the paper he was carrying and presented it to them. Chet grabbed it and examined it.

"They can't do this," he said. "AIDS isn't a contagious disease. It makes no sense to quarantine it."

"It must be contagious," the Sheriff said. "People are catching it."

"A disease is contagious if it can be passed by physical contact, like the measles," Chet said testily. "Or by air, like the common cold. AIDS can't be passed either way."

"Then how do people catch it?"

"Through sexual contact, or from the blood of people who have it."

"How did you folks get it? If you don't mind my asking?"

Chet shook his head and started to say something but Maureen cut in.

"Blood transfusions," she said quickly.

The Sheriff's eyes darted suspiciously between them but he didn't pursue it.

"The entire family was born without the protein that causes blood to clot," Maureen went on. "It's called hemophilia."

"I'm familiar with it," the Sheriff said. "A paper cut could make you bleed to death."

"The only treatment for it is a concentrate made from the blood of normal donors. But they never used to screen donors for the AIDS virus and nearly everybody who used it got infected."

"That's tragic," the Sheriff said. "I'm sorry."

"But there is no known case of the AIDS virus being passed in any other way."

"No *known* case?" the Sheriff said. "That means it's still possible to pass in other ways. The good people of Mittenville are terrified of that happening. They don't want their children infected so they've instructed me to post a quarantine notice on this property."

"That's outrageous," Chet said. "This isn't being done anywhere, not even in Africa where AIDS is epidemic."

"Maybe it should have been," the Sheriff said.

"How long will we be quarantined?" Maureen asked.

"Until everybody's cured."

"Cured?" Chet said. "That's absurd! AIDS is incurable!"

"Does that mean people can't come here anymore?" Maureen asked.

"It's aimed mostly at church and school," the Sheriff said.

"You mean the children are barred from going to church and school?"

"That's the intent."

"They can't do this!" Chet said. "It's unconstitutional!"

"Well they've done it," the Sheriff said. "And it's my duty to see that you observe the quarantine, such as it is, and keep your little ones home."

"What about their Christmas plays?" Maureen said. "They've been rehearsing for weeks!"

"I'm sorry," the Sheriff said. "The order is effective immediately."

Chet could barely contain his fury.

"And I'll bet you just love doing your duty!" he snarled into the Sheriff's face.

"Not always," the Sheriff said backing away. "But

until you can prove to a court that you're being deprived of your constitutional rights, I have to do it. I'm sorry."

The Sheriff smiled awkwardly, put on his Mountie hat and went out. Chet watched him staple the notice to the post on the porch. Then the Sheriff got into his car and drove away.

"He's sorry!" Chet said. "Those unfeeling hypocrites!" He turned to say something more to Maureen but tears were streaming down her face.

"How am I going to tell the kids they can't be in their Christmas plays?" she said.

Chet sat down beside her.

"I'm sorry honey," he said. "We'll think of something." But then he suddenly stood up. "No we won't!" he said. "We'll fight! We'll ignore the quarantine and go to the plays anyway! Let them try and stop us!"

"And have everybody walk out?"

"Let them walk!"

Chet sat down again.

"Quarantined!" he said and banged the armrest in frustration. "Who do they think they are?"

"Frightened people concerned about the well-being of their kids," Maureen said. "I can't really blame them."

"Well I can! Don't they read the papers?"

"I'm afraid they do."

"Of course they do," Chet said calming down.

"That's the problem. Why did you let the Sheriff think we're all infected? If they knew it was only Terry, they might let the twins appear in the play."

Maureen blew her nose in a tissue and shook her head from side to side.

"I can't do that to Terry," she said. "We're either in this together of we're not."

Chet put his arm around her the way he had on the swing before it fell down.

"You're right," he said. "We're in this together."

And he wondered what was going to fall down next.

24

The Sheriff was pulling out of the Alcot's driveway when he saw Sam Slocum pulling in. They stopped opposite each other and rolled down their windows.

"Did you serve that quarantine notice?" Sam Slocum asked.

"Had to."

"I expect you did," Slocum said. "I'm on my way to tell those folks that I'm willing to donate my legal expertise if they care to fight."

"Everybody else is hoping they'll just pack up and leave," the Sheriff said. "Why do you want to get mixed up in something that could get messy?"

"Remember what Edmund Burke said?" Slocum asked.

"Do I know him?"

"You might if you had lived in England two hundred years ago. He said the only thing necessary for the triumph of evil is for good men to do nothing."

The Sheriff digested what he had just heard.

"How's a man supposed to know if he's one of the good ones?" he asked.

"Easy," Slocum said. "His conscience doesn't give him a minute's rest."

He gave the Sheriff a quick wave and drove down to the old house by the lake.

❋ ❋ ❋

25

S am Slocum walked up onto the Alcot's porch and saw the quarantine notice stapled to the post. He pulled it off and rang the doorbell.

When Chet opened the door he said, "My name is Slocum. I was formerly with the Town Council but I resigned over this." He held up the notice. "My legal services are available if you want to challenge it. Gratis, of course."

Chet looked him over.

"You mean there's actually one person in Mittenville who thinks this is wrong?"

"I expect there's more."

"Come in," Chet said. "If you're not afraid to enter the House of AIDS."

"I'm not afraid," Slocum said. "I know a little bit about it."

Chet steered his visitor across the foyer and into the parlor.

"Who is it?" Maureen said still daubing away her tears.

"A Mr. Slocum," Chet said. "He resigned from the Town Council because of our quarantine. Can you believe it? He'd like to know if we're interested in retaining his legal services."

"At no charge," Slocum added. "You should know I've been retired for five years and have no legal staff. So I'm not as up to snuff as I used to be."

"I doubt the Constitution has changed in five years," Chet said.

"I'm pleased to meet you, Mr. Slocum," Maureen said. "We're grateful for your very generous offer but—"

"I'm thrilled at his generous offer!" Chet said. "I want to get those dirtbags real bad, especially the Sheriff."

"Don't misjudge Hobbs," Slocum said. "He's only doing his duty."

"That's what the Nazis said," Chet said. "I say crucify them all."

"Honey, this is Christmas," Maureen said anxiously. "Let's not turn into hypocrites ourselves."

"Tell it to the Town Council," Chet said. "They're the ones who forgot what Christmas is all about. If they ever knew."

"May I get you a cup of coffee, Mr. Slocum?" Maureen asked. "I just made fresh."

"Thank you," Slocum said. "Cream, no sugar. And please call me Sam."

Maureen went into the kitchen while Chet took

Slocum's coat and hung it in the closet. Slocum saw the Christmas tree and went over to it.

"This is a very beautiful tree," he said when Chet came back. "But I'm surprised to see it. I heard you folks didn't celebrate Christmas."

"So now they're trying to demonize us," Chet said. "The sooner we nail those bigots to the wall the better."

"Where is it you'd like to nail them?" Slocum said with mild amusement. "To a cross or to a wall?"

"Frankly, I'm not fussy when it comes to evil people."

Maureen came back with three steaming mugs of coffee. Slocum accepted one and took a sip.

"Nothing like a good cup of coffee," he said. "But you're making a mistake if you think those people are evil."

"What are they if not evil?" Chet said.

"Terrified," Slocum said. "Dealing with the unknown. A frightening prospect for most people, especially if what's at risk is the lives of their children. People don't take chances with their children's lives."

"Why should their children's lives be at risk if ours aren't?" Chet said.

"What do you mean?" Slocum asked.

Chet looked at Maureen who gave him a cautioning stare.

"We weren't going to say anything to anybody,"

Chet said. "But if you're going to represent us you should know. We don't have AIDS. Only our nephew does. He's living with us because his family's been wiped out by the disease."

Slocum stared at them without blinking.

"Your own children don't have it either?" he asked.

"No."

"Yet you've taken the boy into your home?" He shook his head in amazement. "That's incredibly courageous. I feel compelled to salute you."

"It's not all that courageous if there's no risk," Chet said. "We've been living with Terry for years without contracting the virus."

"You're absolutely certain there's no risk?"

"You can't be absolutely certain about anything," Maureen said. "Who knows that better than a lawyer? But risk has to be offset by compassion, or we can't call ourselves members of the human race. Aren't we all in this together?"

"You have my profound admiration too," Slocum said. "You certainly don't deserve what's being visited upon you."

"Right," Chet said. "So how do we get back at them?"

"Is getting back at them as important as making them see the light?"

"They'll never see the light," Chet said. "Their minds are closed."

"Like yours once were?" Slocum asked. "They were, weren't they?"

"Until we found out the facts," Maureen said.

"How did you find them out?"

"We were hit in the face by them when my sister and her husband contracted the disease. They died within three years and Terry had to come live with us. He had nowhere else to go."

"So you didn't just acquire your knowledge through hearsay," Slocum said. "Or by reading about it in the newspaper."

"It was force-fed," Chet admitted.

Slocum leaned forward in his chair.

"Then how can you expect an entire community to learn overnight what it took you years to learn under pressure? Especially if you don't give them all the facts, or show them by example? Aren't you a living example of people who have not been intimidated by the worst disease of the century? Others need to know about you."

"They know, Sam," Chet said. "They had us quarantined."

"That was a knee-jerk reaction," Slocum said. "Don't you share in the blame for keeping the true facts a secret?"

"We did it to protect Terry," Maureen said.

"Maybe that was a mistake," Slocum said.

Chet vigorously shook his head in disagreement.

"I can't believe the people of Mittenville would

131

have accepted us if we had told them up front we had AIDS in the family," he said. "They're too darned prejudiced for that."

"Like you once were," Slocum said.

Chet threw up his hands.

"So what should we do?" he asked. "Go into town and start preaching the truth about AIDS? Sheriff Hobbs will throw us in jail for breaking the quarantine. And you'll end up in jail just for being here."

"Our first order of business is to get a court order suspending the quarantine," Slocum said. "That should be relatively easy."

"Then let's do it," Chet said. "We can show them we're not going to take this lying down."

"Then what?" Maureen said. "Will our kids be welcome in school?"

"I doubt it," Chet said. "The good citizens of Mittenville are probably going to be outraged. But at least they'll know we can't be pushed around."

"So what's that called?" Maureen asked. "A pyrrhic victory?"

Chet looked at her. Suddenly he understood her point of view.

"That's what you don't want, isn't it?" he said, sympathetically. "You don't want to win the battle and lose the war."

"Do you?"

"Not really." Chet turned to Slocum. "Forget the court order. Now what do we do?"

Slocum finished his coffee and stood up.

"Let me think about it," he said. He walked into the foyer to get his coat. "May I see the children before I leave?"

"They're in the library getting ready for their Christmas plays," Maureen said. "We haven't had the heart to burst their bubble."

She opened the doors.

"This is Mr. Slocum," she said to the kids. "He'd like to meet you."

The twins danced over and curtsied.

"I'm Jennifer, the Littlest Angel."

"I'm Suzy. I'm a Littlest Angel too."

"And I'm delighted to meet two such pretty angels," Slocum said.

Terry hobbled over on his crutch.

"I'm Tiny Tim," he said. "This crutch is make-believe. My real name is Terry."

Terry reached out his hand and Slocum stared at it for a moment. He finally shook it.

"I'm delighted to know you, Terry," Slocum said. "The best part of Christmas is the make-believe, isn't it?"

"It sure is!" Terry said.

"There's a lot of truth in it too," Suzy said seriously.

"There is?" Slocum said surprised. "What kind of truth?"

"Everything good happens on account of

Christmas," Suzy said.

"And it doesn't matter what day Jesus was born on as long as he was born," Jennifer said.

"Very good," Slocum said and patted the twins on the head. He took Chet's hand and shook it warmly. "Very good indeed."

They walked to the door.

"Don't spend a lot of time worrying about this," Chet said. "Sounds like our best course of action is to get out of town. We promised Terry we'd find him snow for Christmas."

"Please don't do that before this is settled," Slocum said. "Haven't you read the Farmer's Almanac?"

"No," Chet said. "Why?"

"It says we're going to have a lollapalooza of a white Christmas."

"A lollapalooza?"

"My word, not theirs," Slocum said and patted him on the back as he went out.

26

Chet found some wrapping paper that was left over from last year. By lining it up carefully he was able to cover the entire box.

"I feel guilty about this," he said to Maureen. "The kids should be getting better stuff for Christmas than homemade gifts and IOUs."

"The stores are still open."

"Forget it. We're never going to Mittenville again. Except to drive through on our way out."

"When is that going to be?"

"Probably after Christmas, don't you think? There's no sense even thinking about it before then."

"Have you thought about where we'll go?" Maureen asked.

"Anywhere that's away from here."

"Wherever that is, do you think they'll be more understanding?"

"Probably not."

"Then why leave? At least we've got one friend here."

"What are we supposed to do while we're here?" Chet said throwing down the roll of tape. "This sitting around is driving me nuts."

"Do you still want to confront the people of Mittenville with our situation?" Maureen asked nonchalantly.

"I'd love to see them eat crow, if that's what you mean," Chet said. "Why? What are you driving at?"

"Why don't you start that newspaper the town wants so desperately? It could be our vehicle for getting our story told. And maybe getting some normality back into our lives. I need it, you need it, and so do the kids."

Chet stopped what he was doing and stared off into the distance.

"Interesting idea," he said. "Can you design a sign for us?"

"I'd love to."

"A great big white one that looks like a scroll. You know, nice and literary?"

"Sounds like you've already designed it."

Chet's smile suddenly faded and he went back to taping the package.

"Who are we kidding?" he said. "We haven't got the money."

"Maybe Mr. Slocum can help you get it."

"Why would anybody in this town want to invest in me?"

There was a knock on the bedroom door.

"You can't come in!" Maureen said. "We're busy!"

"It's important," one of the twins said.

"Sounds like Suzy's got a problem," Maureen said and threw a sheet over the gifts on the bed.

"How can you tell them apart?" Chet said.

"Easy," Maureen laughed. "Come in, Suzy."

The door opened and Suzy came in.

"Mr. Ghost is back," she said.

Maureen threw an amused glance at Chet. "Back in the attic?"

"This time he's outside, under the tree."

"Good," Chet said. "We'll lock the door so he can't get back in."

"Locks don't keep ghosts out," Suzy said. "But he looks cold."

"You mean ghosts can get cold?"

Terry came into the room.

"It isn't a ghost," he said and tried to peek under the sheet. "It's only a man."

"Only a man?" Maureen pulled the sheet down. "In our yard?"

"Did you see him?" Chet asked.

"Yup."

"What was he doing?"

"Standing there. Jenn's watching him."

"We'd better go down and check this out," Chet said. "No telling who he might be."

They tumbled down the stairs and pressed their faces up against the parlor window where Jennifer was watching. They could clearly see the tall figure of a man standing like a statue under the great oak.

"I'll be darned," Chet said. "There is somebody out there."

"What do you suppose he wants?" Maureen said.

"Our lives and our fortune."

"Stop being scary," Maureen said. "Try waving to him."

"What for? It'll only encourage him."

Maureen moved her hand across the window in a tentative wave. The man just stood there staring at the house, not moving.

"What's that funny cape he's got on?" she asked.

"That's not a cape," Chet said. "It's a poncho. Protects him from the rain."

"What rain?"

"If we ever get any."

"He looks cold," Jennifer said. "Can we invite him in?"

"No way," Chet said. "How do we know he's not an axe murderer?"

"He's a ghost," Suzy said.

"He isn't a ghost, honey," Chet said. "He's a man. We're looking right at him."

"But that's what the ghost looks like," Jennifer said.

For a fleeting instant Chet recalled the figure he had seen in his dream, standing in front of the French doors. There was a definite resemblance. He was going to say something about it but dismissed the idea.

"Maybe we should invite him in," Maureen said. "After all, it is Christmas."

"That's when they like to strike," Chet said. "Remember what the Sheriff said—Christmas brings out the best."

"If he's up to no good he wouldn't be standing in the open, would he?"

"Maybe he's trying to intimidate us," Terry said.

"That's a pretty big word," Chet said. "Where did you learn it?"

"In a book about a stalker. He would stand outside the house every night where the people could see him just to scare them. Finally he cut off all their heads."

"That's reassuring," Maureen said.

They heard the back door open and close, and heard footsteps on the porch. Chet, Maureen and Terry pressed their faces back to the window. They could see the twins walking hand-in-hand across the porch. While Chet and Maureen stood frozen in terror, the twins walked down the steps and went up to the man.

"Oh my God!" Maureen said as she felt her knees weaken.

"What's wrong with those kids?" Chet said.

"They're stupid!" Terry said. "They're going to get killed!"

139

"Don't say that!" Maureen said. "Chet, do something!"

They could see the twins looking up at the man and talking to him. Then they each took him by the hand and led him back to the house.

"They're bringing him inside!" Chet said.

They watched the twins and the man climb up the steps together and walk across the porch to the kitchen door.

"I told you!" Terry said. "Now we're all going to get killed!"

"Let's not jump to conclusions," Maureen said. "At least we can be hospitable. More than likely he's a homeless old man looking for a hot meal but he's too proud to ask. *I hope!* "

They heard the kitchen door open and close.

"Well, what are we waiting for?" Chet said, reaching for the fireplace poker. "Let's go in and be hospitable."

27

At the door to the kitchen Chet drew Maureen aside.

"I'll insert myself between this dude and the twins," he whispered throatily. "You grab the kids and hustle them into the pantry."

"Why the pantry, for heaven's sake?"

"The door swings in instead of out. You can brace one of the shelves against it. If he overpowers me he won't be able to get at any of you."

"Isn't that a little drastic?" Maureen asked, somewhat horrified.

"I just wish we still had your brother-in-law's shotgun. That's how drastic I think it is."

Chet got a firm grip on the poker and placed his other hand on the swinging door.

"Here goes nothing," he said and pushed his way into the kitchen. Maureen and Terry followed.

They all stopped short. The twins were standing on either side of the man, still holding his hands.

"This is our friend," Jennifer said looking up at

the shadowy figure between her and Suzy. "His name is Okeemakeequid."

At the sound of his name the figure let go of the twins' hands and stepped resolutely into the light.

"He's an Indian!" Chet said putting his arm out and moving them all back a pace.

The Indian's face was brown and leathery, and his graying hair was still shiny black. It was tied in back in a pony tail. He was wearing a heavy cape that looked like a poncho, except it was made of stiff animal hide and had a fringe that went all the way around.

Chet kept a firm grip on the poker and looked back to see if Maureen had made her move. She hadn't. She was transfixed by the apparition before them. Chet turned to face the Indian again, half expecting him to have disappeared.

"Chippewa?" Chet asked when he was sure he was real. He didn't know what else to say.

"Okeemakeequid," the Indian said in a soft, deep voice.

"From the Chippewa reservation?"

"Okeemakeequid!" the Indian said again, this time a little louder.

Chet looked more closely at the Indian. He was old and wizened. He appeared to have been quite tall at one time but now his shoulders were stooped with age.

"He's ancient and harmless," Chet said in an aside

to Maureen. He released the pressure on the poker and slid it behind the cupboard. "You're probably right about the hot meal and being too proud to ask."

"Are you hungry?" Maureen asked. "Are you cold?"

The Indian just stared without reacting in any way. This time Chet asked, only louder and more forcefully.

"Hungry?" he nearly shouted. "Cold?"

There was still no response. Chet decided to try the primitive sign language he had seen in the movies. He pantomimed feeding himself with his hands and then wrapped his arms around himself. The Indian grunted and squatted down on the floor behind the wood-burning stove.

"Well that worked," Chet said. "Now what?"

"Let's make him some popcorn," Suzy said.

"If he's hungry he'll need more than popcorn," Maureen said. "We have some leftover potato salad and chicken."

"Indians like popcorn," Jennifer said.

"How do you know that?" Maureen asked.

"He told us," Jennifer said.

"I thought he didn't understand the language?" Chet said.

"We asked him if he'd like to come in and have some popcorn and he said yes," Suzy said.

"All right," Maureen said, "we'll make him some

popcorn. But I'll put out the chicken and salad just in case."

Chet and Terry went back into the parlor with the bowl and some popping corn while Maureen and the twins got out the leftovers.

"You think he's a real Indian?" Terry asked Chet, his eyes as wide as saucers.

"Looks real to me," Chet said. "I just hope he doesn't eat all the chicken."

"Awesome!" Terry said. "I've never seen a real Indian. I wonder if he's a Medicine Man."

"Could be. Why?"

"Maybe he can make it snow."

"I've heard of a rain dance," Chet said, "but I've never heard of a snow dance."

"Is it all right if I ask him?"

"If you can figure out how to ask him, go right ahead and ask him. We sure don't have anything to lose."

Chet filled the popper and held it over the fire. The kernels started to burst and bang against the copper lid.

"If he's a real Indian," Terry asked, "how come he likes popcorn?"

"We don't know that he does," Chet said. "Maybe he didn't understand the twins. But why shouldn't he like it? The Indians probably invented it. They were growing maize long before Columbus discovered America."

"What's maize?"

"Corn," Chet said. "The stuff that explodes into popcorn."

They filled the bowl and took it into the kitchen. Maureen had set the leftovers out on a small table near the Indian so Chet put the bowl down next to them. The Indian greedily took a handful of warm popcorn and stuffed it into his mouth.

"Must be the butter," Chet said. "We put on lots of butter."

Chet motioned for everybody to follow him and held the swinging door open while they filed out.

"What are we going to do with him?" Maureen said when they were in the parlor and out of earshot.

"Let's keep him," Suzy said.

"He's not a stray cat," Chet said. "After he eats he leaves."

"We can't send him back out there," Maureen said.

"That's where he came from," Chet said. "He can't stay here."

"Why not?"

"Where's he going to sleep?"

"In the attic," Jennifer said. "Where we saw him first."

"It's too cold up there," Chet said. "He'll freeze to death. We'll have a dead Indian on our hands and Sheriff Hobbs will lock us up for life."

"He'll be okay," Suzy said. "Ghosts can't freeze."

"He's not a ghost, dummy," Terry said. "Didn't you see him eating popcorn?"

"Ghosts can eat anything they want to," Suzy said.

"Boy!" Terry said disgustedly. "Girls are really dumb!"

"We have an extra bedroom," Jennifer said. "Can't he sleep there?"

"No, honey," Chet said. "We can't have a stranger sleeping with us upstairs. It's too dangerous." He looked at their suddenly mournful faces and capitulated. "If he stays he'll have to stay in the kitchen."

"Goody!" the twins said.

"He can't sleep on the floor like a dog," Maureen said.

"He looked pretty comfortable to me," Chet said. "But if it'll make you feel better I'll bring down a cot and he can sleep in the pantry."

"Why the pantry again?"

"For one thing, there's nothing in there he can steal. And the door can be locked from the outside."

Maureen looked at Chet in disbelief. "You're going to lock him in?"

"Yes. I'd like to sleep tonight too."

"What if he has to go to the bathroom?"

"There's a pail in there."

"Chet, that's gross. And he's an old man."

"Those are my conditions," Chet said adamantly. "Terry and I have two gorgeous daughters and a beautiful wife to protect and we're going to protect them, like it or not. Isn't that right, sport?"

"That's right!" Terry said firmly.

"Okeemakeequid won't hurt us," Suzy said. "He likes us."

Chet smiled and stroked Suzy's hair.

"He likes you because you can pronounce his name, pumpkin. But don't let it go to your cute little head. I can pronounce it too." Chet made out as if he was taking a deep breath. "Okefenokee-fenee-quog!" he said.

"Wrong!" the twins said in unison.

"Let me try," Maureen said. She closed her eyes and said, "The Okey-dokey-fenokee kid."

"Wrong!" the twins said again and jumped up and down with delight.

"It's Okeemakeequid!" Terry said proudly.

"Very good," Maureen said in amazement. "That's a very difficult and unusual name. How did you remember it so well?"

"It sounds like the name of a real Medicine Man," Terry added. "I like it!"

28

Chet was going to go into town without breakfast but decided he needed a little something
to fortify himself. He went into the kitchen and was
pouring himself a glass of orange juice when he saw
that the pantry door was open.

"I know I locked that door," he said and looked
into the pantry.

The cot was in there, and so were the pillow and
blankets, but no Indian. Chet went over to the small
table and picked up the plate of leftovers. The
potato salad was still there but the chicken was gone.

"Good riddance," he said glumly. "At least they
can't blame me for kicking the old buzzard out."

Chet finished his juice and drove the psychedelic
pie-van into town. He stopped in front of a vacant
storefront on Main Street and copied down the
name and number posted there. Then he drove over
to Sam Slocum's office which was really Sam
Slocum's house. By now, he was sure, telephones all
over Mittenville were ringing.

"How bad does this town want a newspaper?" Chet asked Slocum over a cup of instant coffee.

"We've never had one," Slocum said. "As you might imagine, we'd like to have one real bad. Why?"

"Bad enough to rent me the space and sell me enough supplies to get one started?"

"That's a horse of a different color," Slocum said. "When it comes to business, Mittenville is no different from any other town in America. There is no prejudice here against profit, and no quarantine on money."

"A matter of principle?" Chet grinned.

"A matter of survival," Slocum said. "This town is hard-up."

"All I need to get started is an old copy machine," Chet said. "I already have an old manual typewriter. I can start by printing one sheet per issue and then work up to two sheets. It won't look like *The New York Times* but it'll be all the news that's fit to print."

"I've got an old mimeograph in the basement," Slocum said. "It's slow and messy but it'll make copies all day long."

"What does it take to run one?"

"Me," Slocum said and leaned back in his chair. "I can also supply the office furniture. I've got a basement full that I've been dying to get rid of."

"You wouldn't consider becoming a partner, would you?" Chet asked.

"I might," Slocum said. "Now that I'm a widower

with time on my hands. Why don't you try asking me?"

Chet adopted a proper stance and a professional tone.

"Mr. Slocum," he said seriously. "Would you consider becoming a partner with a certain Mr. C. Alcot who desires to establish Mittenville's first real newspaper?"

Slocum made like he was thinking it over.

"Don't mind if I do," he finally said. "Let's drink on it."

They clinked their coffee mugs together.

"Here's to the Mittenville—" Slocum paused. "What are we going to call it?"

"I've already thought of that, if you approve. *The Mittenville Chronicle.* Sounds important without being pompous."

"*The Mittenville Chronicle,*" Slocum said, letting each word roll off his tongue. "I like the way it sounds. I approve."

They clinked their coffee mugs together again.

"Unfortunately, I can only afford one month's rent," Chet said. He took a piece of paper out of his pocket and looked at it. "Do you think this Mr. Forbush will rent me his store for that short a time?"

"Forbush?" Slocum grinned. "He'd rent it to the pope for that short a time. But since we're partners I'll put up another month's rent and get him to sign a three-year lease. He'll jump at it."

"Terrific," Chet said. "Let's do it."

"For three years?" Slocum said. "That's quite a commitment to this community. Are you prepared to make it?"

"It's probably going to take me that long to change these people's minds about us," Chet said. "The sooner we get started the better."

Sam Slocum got Forbush to agree to the deal over the phone. He left to get it in writing while Chet drove back down Main Street and stopped in front of the vacant storefront. As people in neighboring stores watched, Chet took a large white sign out of the van and hung it on the hooks above the door. Then Chet stepped back to admire it. The beautiful gold and black lettering said:

The Mittenville Chronicle
C. Alcot, Publisher

29

Maureen came out on the porch when she heard Chet drive up. She was bursting with anticipation.

"Did you do it?"

"I did it," he said. "I hung out the shingle."

Maureen threw her arms around him.

"I love you for doing it!" she said. "It's a real aggressive move that shows everybody we're not going to be stampeded out."

"I hope Mittenville is going to love me as much as you do," Chet said. "Slocum's our partner in the deal so that might help."

"Wonderful! This is really a new beginning for us, isn't it?"

"As long as that crusty old Sheriff doesn't throw me in jail. The whole town watched me put up the sign."

"How did it look?"

"Beautiful, hon. You did a great job. With luck it'll be up for three years. That's how long the lease is for."

"That means we don't have to move!" Maureen said clapping her hands.

"I'm not so sure," Chet said. "The lease may be good for three years but I don't know if we are. We're pushing them pretty hard."

"They'll come around," Maureen said. "If they want a newspaper bad enough, this will force them to face reality and do the right thing—for the town and for us."

"I wish I had as much faith in human nature as you have," Chet said. "By the way, I didn't boot old Okee out the door. He was already gone by the time I came down."

"I know," Maureen said cheerfully. "He went down to the lake with the kids."

"And you let them go?"

"That old man wouldn't hurt a fly," Maureen said. "The kids have taken to him like they would to their own grandfather."

"He's kind of old and leathery for a grandfather, isn't he?"

"All grandfathers are."

Chet noticed a spiral of smoke curling up into the sky on the other side of the lake.

"What's that," he said pointing to it. "A fire?"

"Probably Okee and the kids," Maureen said. "There's nobody else out there."

"I wonder if they're burning that special wood."

"If anybody's entitled to burn it, Okee certainly is."

"I guess he is," Chet said. "I hope he isn't staying for dinner."

"Of course he's staying for dinner. Christmas dinner too if he wants to. We're not kicking anybody out at this time of year."

"Indians are heathen," Chet said. "They don't believe in Christmas."

"Well I believe in it," Maureen said. "And so do you. And you know how much I like to have people around for the holidays."

"Yes but strangers?" Chet groaned. "Why can't we politely ask him to leave? I'll even take him to the reservation if I have to."

"Dear," Maureen said with great forbearance, "if it wasn't for this stranger, we'd be all alone. We're quarantined, remember? Let's be thankful for God's little favors."

Chet conceded with a weary wave.

"Okay," he said. "But God's little favor stays in the pantry."

"He doesn't seem to mind," Maureen said.

"It's better than a teepee, that's why. But right after Christmas, out he goes."

"Right after Twelfth Night."

"When is that?" Chet said with a pained expression.

"January the fifth. Everybody knows that."

Chet exhaled loudly in a way that sounded more like a groan.

"That's what I meant," he said. "Right after Twelfth Night."

❄ ❄ ❄

30

Terry and the twins huddled by the fire while the old Indian went off by himself and stood staring at the lake.

"He didn't use a match," Suzy said. "Just rubbed those sticks together and the wood started to burn."

"Indians know exactly what kind of wood to use and how to rub it," Terry said. "It's a secret they never share with palefaces."

"What's a paleface?" Suzy asked.

"We are," Terry said showing them the back of his hand. "Can't you tell?"

"Are you going to ask him to make it snow?" Jennifer said.

Terry shrugged.

"Dad says there's a dance to make it rain, but he's never heard of a dance to make it snow."

"It doesn't matter," Suzy said. "If it's cold enough the rain will turn to snow."

Terry brightened. "That's right!" he said.

He threw the stick he was holding into the fire

and walked over to the old Indian. The twins got up and followed.

"Okeemakeequid?" Terry said to the old man.

The old man turned around. His leathery face was impassive but his eyes seemed to be smiling. Terry was suddenly panic-stricken.

"I don't know what to do next!" Terry whispered to the twins. "How do I ask him?"

"Try sign language, the way dad did!" Jennifer whispered back.

Terry thought about that. "How do you do rain in sign language?"

"I don't know," Suzy whispered. "This is how we do snow in ballet."

She stretched her arms out and brought them down slowly while she wiggled her fingers.

"That's it!" Terry said in a loud whisper. "I'll try it!"

He stood up straight and raised his hand in a sign to the Indian.

"Okeemakeequid?" he said.

The old man looked down again.

"Make snow!" Terry said, enunciating carefully and distinctly.

He stretched his arms out and brought them down while he wiggled his fingers.

"For me!" Terry said and touched his fist to his chest. And then he added, "Pretty please?"

The old Indian made no response.

"He didn't understand!" Terry whispered to the twins.

157

"Let's all try it!" Suzy whispered.

The three of them raised their arms and slowly brought them down while they wiggled their fingers.

"Sno-o-o-ow! they said in ragged unison.

When there was still no response Terry flapped his hand against his mouth the way kids do to imitate Indians, and danced in a circle. The old Indian watched him for a while, then tipped his head back and let out a strange raucous howl that turned out to be a laugh.

"Ka-wa-skin-ne-ka!" the Indian said nodding his head and laughing at the same time. "Ka-wa-skin-ne-ka!"

"What does that mean?" Jennifer asked Terry.

"I don't know," Terry said, "But it sounds good!" He raised his arm in a salute and repeated, "Ka-wa-skin-ne-ka!"

Okeemakeequid turned around to face the lake and extended his arms out in front of him. He lowered his head and started to sing slowly and mournfully. As he sang, the song got louder and his head lifted to the sky.

"It's working!" Terry said to the twins. "He's going to make it snow! I know he is!"

Then Terry and the twins turned their faces up into the sky and watched for the snow they were sure was about to fall.

❄ ❄ ❄

31

Sam Slocum showed up uninvited to the special meeting of the Town Council and sat in his regular chair. Nine pair of eyebrows shot up around the table.

"What are you doing here?" Mudge said sourly. "You resigned."

"He did resign," Buxton said through a frown. "Told us we were all asses and said he didn't want to have anything to do with us or our resolution."

"I changed my mind about some of those things," Slocum said amiably. "That's why I decided to withdraw my resignation."

"Can he do that?" Denby asked the Chairman.

Chairman Bisbee peered over his glasses.

"Until I receive his resignation in writing, as prescribed by the bylaws," Bisbee said, "he's still an official member of this body."

"Saved by a technicality," Mudge grunted.

Reverend Hipwood knocked on the door and tentatively stuck his head into the room.

"Mr. Chairman," he said to Bisbee, "this is not my bailiwick. But I heard about the breach of quarantine. With your sufferance I would like to monitor the proceedings."

"Come in, Wilbur," Bisbee said. "We're about to delve into that very subject. Bring Hobbsie with you."

Reverend Hipwood and the Sheriff came in and Bisbee brought the meeting to order by tapping his coffee cup with a pencil.

"Our first and only order of business," Bisbee said, "is to ask Sheriff Hobbs what he's planning to do about the flouting of our quarantine. And as soon as the Sheriff sits down we'll ask him."

Sheriff Hobbs sat down with a scowl and swiveled his chair to face the Chairman.

"Well, Sheriff?" Bisbee said. "You heard the question. What are you going to do about it? You were supposed to enforce that order."

Before the Sheriff got a word out of his mouth Mudge spoke up.

"And what about Forbush renting his place to Alcot?" he said. "That adds insult to injury."

The Sheriff swiveled to face Mudge.

"It is not against the law to rent anything to anybody," he said, "as long as the rented property is used for lawful purposes. A newspaper fits the definition of lawful purposes, as I understand it."

"What newspaper?" Buxton said. "All we've seen

160

so far is a sign. It could be a front for drugs."

"Or pies!" Denby said and shared a laugh with some of the others.

"Before you say anything else," the Sheriff said, "I think you need to hear what I found out from the authorities in Dearborn."

"Dug up some dirt, did you, Hobbsie?" Mudge said.

"Just the opposite," the Sheriff said. He paused until he had everybody's undivided attention. "I found out the Alcot family doesn't have AIDS at all."

Subdued muttering encircled the table.

"What do you mean, they don't have it?" the Chairman asked.

"Just what I said," the Sheriff said. "Only the boy has it, and he's adopted."

"That still means there's AIDS in that family," Denby said. "That's what we were concerned about in the first place."

"And it's still contagious," Mudge said. "So what else is new?"

"If it's so contagious," the Sheriff said, "doesn't it seem odd to you that the Alcots were not afraid to bring that child into their own home, and expose themselves and their natural children to it?"

"They're reckless," Denby said. "All the more reason they need to be quarantined."

"I don't think they're reckless at all," the Sheriff said. "I think they know they can't catch it."

"How do they know that?" Buxton said.

Sheriff Hobbs took out a sheet of paper and snapped it open.

"I contacted the Centers for Disease Control in Atlanta," he said. "They faxed me the most recent data on AIDS. It can be summarized as follows." He put on his glasses and squinted at the paper. "The virus that causes AIDS cannot be transmitted through routine contact."

The Sheriff took off his glasses.

"I repeat," he said loudly and slowly while he glared at the others in the room. "The virus that causes AIDS cannot be transmitted through routine contact!"

"What about sneezing and coughing?" Mudge said.

"Or kissing?" Buxton said.

"Or spitting?" Denby said. "I read about a man being arrested for attempted murder because he had AIDS and was spitting on people."

"I happened to ask about that particular case," the Sheriff said. "The CDC said spitting is not a factor in transmitting the AIDS virus. Neither is touching. Which is why quarantining is uncalled-for and is, in fact, improper and illegal."

"Says who?" Mudge asked with some annoyance.

"Says I!" the Sheriff said indignantly. "The American Red Cross, whom I also contacted, informs me that not one case of AIDS is known to have been transmitted in school. They say a student cannot get AIDS by sitting next to somebody who has it."

"Are you telling me we should cancel the quarantine?" Mudge said, his head cocked aggressively. "All because of a scrap of paper from some Federal bureaucracy?"

"We can't cancel the quarantine," Buxton said. "The people who sent that paper live in Atlanta. We live in Mittenville and have to face the music."

Sheriff Hobbs suddenly got up from his chair and slapped the table with his hand. The loud noise jolted everybody to attention.

"I've got a mind to throw the bunch of you in jail!" he said. "You acted impulsively, without giving due cause or consideration to the propriety or impact of your decision! You can't do this and you should have known you can't!"

"We're the Town Council," Bisbee said officiously. "We can do anything we want."

"Not as long as I'm here," the Sheriff said. "Your actions have to comply with the letter of the law, and me. And that quarantine doesn't do either."

"So what if it's technically improper?" Mudge said. "Who cares?"

"I care!" the Sheriff said. "It makes me look like a sloppy lawman, and I don't like that. I am meticulous!" He slapped the table again.

The council looked at one another in chagrined silence.

"I'd like to add something to what the Sheriff said," Slocum said.

There was a sigh of annoyance from some members but Slocum ignored them and got to his feet anyway.

"This town is going to have to learn to deal with a very deadly disease," he said. "Not because Terry Alcot has it, but because somebody close to you is also going to get it."

"I refuse to accept that," Mudge snapped.

"That's an outrageous accusation," Denby said.

"Let's not delude ourselves," Slocum said. "Our loved ones live in this world too. Some of them will get AIDS no matter how righteously they conduct themselves, no matter how carefully they lead their lives. And when they get it they're going to need medical care, and you're going to have to know how to deal with it."

"And you're being ridiculous," Buxton said. "This isn't Detroit or San Francisco."

"In a way it is," Slocum said. "We are vulnerable to the same seven deadly sins they are. God hasn't exempted us from drugs or sins of the flesh. He won't exempt us from this disease either. This is its first visit. We should think of it as an early warning, and learn from it."

"The lesson is not to sanction disease," Buxton said, "but to keep our town wholesome and pure."

"The lesson is to recognize AIDS for what it is

and what it isn't," Slocum said. "The Alcots found a way to do that, through courage, understanding and love. These are virtues all Christians should aspire to, aren't they Reverend?"

"They are indeed," the Reverend said. "But what about the moral question? The two are inextricably intertwined. Our goal was to protect our children from pagan influences. And as one of you said, AIDS is a curse of God that smites the wicked and the children of the wicked."

"I said that," Denby said haughtily. "And I'll say it again."

"Save your breath," Slocum said. "In this case AIDS was a curse of man, visited upon the innocent. Terry and his original family got the disease while being treated for hemophilia. The rest of the family is already dead through no sin of their own. There's nothing wicked or pagan about the Alcots, Reverend. They appear to be more religious than many of us, and more compassionate than most."

"But we have heard their testaments from the lips of the children!" a suddenly perplexed Reverend Hipwood said. "They have taken issue with fundamental Christian gospels like the story of the Nativity!"

"Which gospel?" Slocum said. "Matthew's? In which three wise men follow the star to Bethlehem? Or Luke's, which doesn't mention the wise men but has shepherds finding the babe in a manger that

165

Matthew takes no notice of? Or Mark's and John's, which skip over all of that?"

"We mustn't get lost in the details," the Reverend said. "It's the greater truth that is sacred."

"I agree," Slocum said. "Which is what the Alcots told their children, and their children told our children, and our children told us. But we were blinded by their candor. Imagine, telling children to believe in truth, not fact. To believe in the spirit of the law, not the letter." He shook his head sadly and added in a low voice, "Disgraceful, isn't it?"

Slocum waited for a reaction but there was none. Most of the members of the Council were staring at the table.

"Perhaps we haven't been teaching our children as well as the Alcots have been teaching theirs," Slocum continued. "Not only have we unjustly ostracized them from our community for it, we've also libeled them. As a lawyer, I should advise you that you could be liable for damages if the Alcots choose to bring charges."

"So that's your game," Mudge said looking up. "Getting a nice retainer to help pay for a retirement condo in Fort Myers?"

"My services have been offered to them free," Slocum said. "After all, it is Christmas. But my real game is fairness. I'd like to see them treated the same way we'd treat our own families. They deserve a medal from this community, not banishment."

Chairman Bisbee cleared his throat.

"What about The Mittenville Chronicle?" he asked. "Do you think it represents a bona fide newspaper? Or is Alcot just playing games?"

"If anybody's playing games, Mr. Chairman," Slocum said, "this Council is. Leave the poor man alone so he can run his newspaper, and do us a favor! It's nearly Christmas, isn't it? Why don't we try acting like it is?"

The Council broke up into small groups that huddled to discuss the issues. Reverend Hipwood walked over to Sam Slocum and dropped his head in humility.

"It is mortifying for me, a man of the cloth," the Reverend said, "to be taking a lesson in spirituality from you, a man of the world."

"I don't think I said anything you haven't already said from your pulpit," Slocum said.

"I'm afraid you did," Reverend Hipwood said. "Sometimes we get so close to the letter of the gospel that we miss its meaning."

"And to the law," Slocum said. "I must admit I've done that myself."

"Thank you for helping us see the light," the Reverend said. "We should have been able to see it in the beginning." His face twisted in an anxiety of doubt. "I don't know why we didn't. Why didn't I see it, of all people? I should have led the way. I not only failed myself and the community, I failed the

Alcots—and that poor little boy."

Sam Slocum laid his hand on the Reverend's shoulder.

"If we were able to see everything in the beginning and recognize it instantly," Slocum said, "there'd never be a need for redemption. Yet redemption is one of life's most uplifting experiences."

The Reverend looked into Sam Slocum's eyes as if he was searching for something.

"I had always believed I had been given the gift of righteousness," he said. "But now, when I see it in someone like you, I know how poor in spirit I really am."

Sheriff Hobbs came up to them in time to hear the last part of what the Reverend had said.

"If you want to see somebody poor in spirit," the Sheriff winked, "keep your eye on this bunch if they don't raise that quarantine. Those jail cells can feel awfully cold and lonely on Christmas Eve."

32

Terry and the twins stared unwaveringly out the window.

"I don't see any snow," Suzy said.

"He's working on it," Terry said.

Maureen came into the parlor with a steaming wassail bowl.

"Look what I've got!" she said brightly.

But the kids barely looked at her.

"What's going on?" Maureen asked.

"Nothing."

"Where's Okee?"

"Under the tree," Terry said.

"What's he doing out there? It's starting to get dark."

"Sitting under his poncho."

Piqued by the partial answers, Maureen went to the window and looked for herself. She could barely make out the pyramid shape under the old oak tree.

"Isn't it too chilly for him to be doing that?" she said. "Whatever it is he's doing?"

He's trying to make it snow," Terry said.

"Why can't he do it from in here where it's warm?"

"Indians need to work under the sky," Terry said with disdain.

"We tried to bring him in," Jennifer said, "but he just sat down and wrapped himself in that old leather blanket."

Chet brought in the popcorn fixings.

"The smell of this will soon bring that old Indian in," he said. "How about it, kids? Who wants to jiggle the popper?"

The kids just shrugged.

Chet looked at Maureen who also shrugged.

"Why is everybody so cheerful on Christmas Eve?" he asked.

"They're waiting for it to snow," Maureen said.

"Snow? It isn't even freezing out there."

"We asked Okee to do a snow dance and he did one for us," Suzy said.

"It was more of a song," Terry corrected. "He called it Ka-wa-skin-ne-ka. I think it's a medicine song."

Chet leaned over Terry's shoulder and looked up at the dark sky. He hoped that something would start to fall but nothing did.

"The watched pot never boils," Maureen said.

"That's right," Chet said. "Why don't we give old Okee a chance and move over to the fireplace? I brought tons of butter."

They gathered around the fireplace and popped popcorn by the bushel. They washed most of it down with gallons of wassail. Then they sang Christmas carols until the kids got sleepy. At that point Chet fanned a yawn and looked at his watch.

"I think it's time we went to bed," he said. "Santa will be making his rounds soon."

A faint jingle of sleigh bells came from upstairs. The twins' mouths fell open and they looked at each other in wide-eyed wonder.

"It's him!" Suzy said. "It's Santa!"

"Better get to bed," Maureen said. "Santa doesn't stop if the kids are still up."

The twins excitedly kissed Chet and Maureen and ran upstairs. Terry remained blasé. He warily circled Chet while staring at the floor where Chet was sitting.

"What are you looking for?" Chet asked.

"I know you rang those bells," Terry said. "How did you do it?"

"It's time for you to get to bed too," Maureen said. "Last year you were up at four to open your presents."

"That's when I was young and used to believe in Santa Claus," Terry said as he slouched into the foyer. "This year I believe in Indians so I'm getting up at four to see it snow." He held his hand up in a salute. "Ka-wa-skin-ne-ka," he said and disappeared up the stairs.

Maureen leaned over to Chet.

"How did you do it?" she asked.

"I don't know what you mean," he said, keeping a straight face. "I think that really was Santa Claus."

"Sure it was, Maureen said. "And I saw mommy kissing him."

She kissed Chet while she reached behind him and found the thread.

"That was sneaky!" Chet said.

She followed the thread under the rug, along the floorboards and up to the window. She gave it a pull. Upstairs, sleigh bells rang.

"You're amazing," she said. "Nobody who'd go to all this trouble for Christmas Eve could possibly be the old Scrooge you pretend to be."

"I'm not old!" Chet said.

Maureen glanced out the window.

"Think we should check on the old man before we retire?"

"Why?" Chet said. "He knows enough to come in out of the cold."

"What if he's too sick to come in? Old men get sick from the cold."

"Not that old man. He's probably weathered a hundred winters."

"All the same, he shouldn't be out there by himself. It's Christmas."

"That's what people always say when they want

you to do something you don't want to do," Chet said. He got up and went to the closet. "Well? Are you going out there with me?"

They put on their coats and slipped outside. They glanced up at the windows to make sure the kids' faces weren't pressed to the glass, then walked over to the leather blanket Okee had wrapped himself in.

"Okee, are you in there?" Chet said, tapping on the stiff hide.

Chet cocked his head and listened. From inside the makeshift tent he could hear the faint drone of Okee's voice, and a phrase he thought he recognized.

"Ka-wa-skin-ne-ka," the old Indian said. Then there was nothing.

"What did he say?" Maureen asked.

"That he didn't want to come inside."

"Seriously."

"He said that funny word that Terry used. Ka-wa-skin-something."

"At least we know he's alive," Maureen said.

"They've lived under these hides for generations," Chet said. "They know how to stay warm."

A light rain started to fall. Chet held out his hand and felt the tiny drops hitting his palm.

"Okee must be doing his thing."

The rain suddenly grew intense and pelted them with stinging drops until they ran up onto the porch.

"He's going to get soaked," Maureen said.

They looked back at the pyramid. The old Indian had drawn it up over his head into the shape of a perfect teepee.

"He'll be all right," Chet said. "If he turned the rain on he knows how to turn it off. It's probably just another one of those brief cloud bursts that never lasts."

They went inside and hung up their coats. They tiptoed up the stairs and went into the bedroom where the gifts were piled. Maureen pulled off the sheet and made some final adjustments to the ribbons and bows. Then they gathered up the gifts and stole back downstairs.

"I hope the kids won't be disappointed," Chet said.

They stacked the big packages under the tree and stuffed the little ones in the stockings that hung over the fireplace.

"They won't be," Maureen said. "This is all pretty wonderful. Thank you for helping to make it so."

She kneeled down beside him and gave him a kiss. Then she rested her head on his shoulder. The candles had burned down low and the fireplace was aglow with shimmering embers.

"Can I ask you something?" Chet said.

Maureen raised her head and looked at him.

"Of course you can. What?"

"Do you think wishes ever come true?"

She smiled. "They do if you wish hard enough."

"Good," he said, "because I'm wishing hard."

"For snow?"

"For Terry. More than anything, I want him to be all right."

"He'll be all right," Maureen said. "At this magical time of year, wishes really can come true."

There was no doubt in her voice, but there was a glimmer of doubt in her eyes which she was just as glad Chet couldn't see.

❄ ❄ ❄

33

Chet woke up with a start. For an instant he thought he saw a man standing at the foot of the bed. It was the middle of the night. Rain was hammering the roof and lashing the windows. He padded across the cold floor and looked out. Water was cascading off the roof in sheets and running across the ground in rivulets. Okee's tent, barely visible through the torrential downpour, glistened wet in the darkness. Chet climbed back into bed, curled up under the warmth of the covers and slept fitfully.

High in the night sky the jet stream shifted slowly southward. It brought with it a northern high that overpowered the southern low. The driving rain turned into cutting sleet. As the temperature dropped, the sleet turned into ice crystals. The crystals melted when they hit the ground but eventually the ground cooled and the crystals formed a crusty layer of ice.

The wind grew stronger and chilled the crystals, stealing away the moisture that caused them to stick together. They became nuggets of ice that ran before the wind and accumulated in corrugated drifts. The drifts grew until they embraced the trees, flowed over the hills and stretched across the roads in great white barriers.

At the same time, the lake froze from the outside in. Ducks seeking the last measure of warmth followed the creeping ice to the huge circle of water in the center. But soon even the center froze and only a flat snow pan remained on which the fowl huddled in quiet resignation.

When the wind died the drifting stopped. In the silence of the night falling crystals collided with one another and formed giant snowflakes. They fell like feathers in endless procession, piling atop one another until at dawn the world lay carpeted under a thick blanket of white.

Terry and the twins burst into Maureen and Chet's room.

"It's snowing!" Terry shouted and danced around the room.

"He did it!" the twins said. "He did it!".

"Who did what?" Chet groaned.

"Look outside!" Terry said.

Maureen pulled the quilt up over her head.

Chet crawled out of bed and staggered over to the window. He rubbed a hole in the frost.

"Holy mackerel!" he said as he took it all in.

From the roof of the house, heavy white forelocks

of snow drooped over the eaves like the billowy white drapes of some magical theater. Evergreens displayed coats of white ermine, and even the bare oaks were dressed in white. The utility poles all wore jaunty white caps, and the electrical wires carried strings of white fluff except where the birds had broken it with their feet.

Terry and the twins grabbed Chet's hands and the four of them danced in a circle.

"It's here! It's here!"

Maureen finally moaned and peeked out from under the quilt. "What's here? What's going on?"

"Honey, you've got to see this!" Chet said.

He threw the covers off her and half-carried her to the window. She wriggled free and held up her hands to hold everybody off so her groggy brain could came around. When it finally did, she put her eye up to the hole and looked out. The others waited expectantly for her reaction.

"My heavens!" she said in stunned amazement. "A winter wonderland!"

They grabbed her hands and danced her in a circle.

"It's here! It's here! The Christmas snow is here!"

"Where did it all come from?" Maureen asked.

"Okee did it!" Terry said. "I'm going out to play in it!"

He tore out of the room and the twins ran after him.

"Do you realize what this means?" Chet said to

Maureen. "Terry's Christmas wish has come true!"

"Merry Christmas, darling," Maureen said. She was now fully awake and stood on her toes to give him a kiss. "Didn't I say everything would turn out all right?"

"Merry Christmas and how!" Chet said. "What did you say it would have to be? A miracle? Well this is some kind of miracle! Last night it was warm enough to go swimming. Today the world is buried under two feet of snow!"

"Do you think Okee really had something to do with it?"

"Who knows!" Chet said rubbing another peep-hole in the frost. "I wonder how the old guy's doing?"

They peeked out. Only the tip of Okee's little tent showed through the drifted snow.

"We'd better go out and make sure he's all right," Chet said.

They dressed in warm winter clothes and hurried downstairs. Terry and the twins had ignored the gifts under the tree and were already out on the front porch diving into the snowbanks. Chet and Maureen went to the back door and opened it. Their way was blocked by a drift that came up to their waists.

"I'll bet we got three feet," Chet said.

"I'll get the yardstick," Maureen said, and went back to the pantry.

Chet charged into the huge drift and broke a trail for Maureen to follow. The going was heavy. He could barely push his feet through the deep snow. Maureen came out and stabbed a yardstick into it.

"Twenty-seven inches!" she called out.

"Holy cow!" Chet said. "Where did it all come from?"

"I'll bet Okee knows!"

They trudged across the yard step after arduous step until they came to the little tent. It was frozen hard and nearly buried. Chet scooped away the snow.

"This is what probably saved him from the icy wind," he said.

He pried open a corner of the leather blanket and cupped his eyes so he could see inside. He suddenly straightened up.

"What's wrong?" Maureen asked, suppressing a feeling of rising horror.

"He's not in there," Chet said.

"He's got to be! Why isn't he?"

"I don't know," Chet said and looked around. "He must have crawled out in the middle of the night and tried to make it back to the house."

Maureen looked at the house, distraught.

"He's not in the pantry!" she cried. "I was just in there!"

"Good Lord!" Chet said twisting around and staring at the ground. "I hope he's not buried under here somewhere!"

They tramped through the snow for what seemed like hours, pushing through drifts and plunging their arms down to the frozen ground, but the old man was not to be found. Heartsick, they fell back into one of the snowbanks and sat there exhausted. Their breath came out in little white puffs.

"Maybe he went back to where he came from," Chet said.

"Without his blanket? That would be like you not taking your coat."

"The blanket's frozen solid. He probably couldn't move it."

"I hope we don't find him somewhere down the road," Maureen said. "Frozen solid too."

They could see the children on the porch, laughing and waving cheerfully. Chet and Maureen waved back.

"They don't seem too concerned," Maureen said.

"Why would they be?" Chet said. "Their Christmas wish came true."

Reluctantly, they got up and trudged back to the house. They stomped the snow off their boots and hung their jackets in the pantry where the old Indian's cot still stood.

"What do we say to the kids?" Chet said.

"I don't know," Maureen said. "I still don't understand it myself."

Hours later the kids came in with red faces and

runny noses. They shrugged off their clothes and gathered around the Christmas tree while Maureen brought in mugs of hot chocolate.

"We should say something about the old Indian," Chet said quietly to Maureen. "I'm amazed one of them hasn't already asked."

"They're kids," Maureen said. "They're still pre-occupied with the snow, and with Christmas."

"Still, I'd better talk to them," Chet said.

He kneeled down beside the kids.

"I think Okee is—gone," he said, taking it one step at a time.

"We know," Jennifer said happily.

"You know?"

"He told us he was going," Suzy said.

"When?" Maureen asked.

"Last night," Jennifer said. "He was in our room and waved goodbye." She demonstrated by holding her hand up and moving it from side to side.

"I had the same dream," Terry said.

"It wasn't a dream!" Suzy said loudly to Terry. "He was there!"

Chet raised his eyebrows and looked at Maureen who had raised hers.

"So," Chet said to the kids. "Does this mean old Okee's back in the attic?"

"Nope. He's gone," Jennifer said.

"Forever," Suzy said.

"I don't believe in ghosts," Terry said, "but I

believe in Okeemakeequid. I'll never forget him."

"Neither will we!" Maureen said.

Terry started to read the names off the packages when they heard the bluster of snowmobiles in the distance. The sound grew louder as the snowmobiles drew closer. Terry ran to the window.

"I can see them!" he said. "There's three!"

The others went to the window and looked out.

The snowmobiles had circled the lake and were bearing down on the house. On the back of each a blue light was flashing the way they do on police cars. The noisy machines bounded over the drifts and growled up to the porch where they stopped.

Sheriff Hobbs and his two Deputies dismounted. The Sheriff's snowmobile was towing a large sled covered with a tarp.

"Dear God!" Maureen said and looked at Chet.

Chet squeezed her hand.

The Sheriff tugged off the helmet he was wearing and set it down on the seat of the snowmobile. Then he went over to the sled and began untying the tarp.

❄ ❄ ❄

34

While Delmar and Lester watched, Sheriff Hobbs slowly untied the ropes that held the tarp down. When he had them all undone he grabbed the tarp with both hands and whipped it off to reveal a huge stack of Christmas presents. They were beautifully wrapped in paper of every color, with bows of every size and shape.

The Sheriff looked up at the house, saw all the faces pressed to the window and waved. Delmar and Lester waved too.

"Here comes Santy Claus!" the Sheriff shouted. "Open the door so we can haul it all in!"

"Presents!" the kids said and ran to the door and threw it open.

Chet and Maureen came up behind them and stepped out on the porch.

"What's this all about?" Chet said.

"Gifts of the Magi," the Sheriff said dryly. "From the Church Elders and the Town Council. In Mittenville everybody who's anybody's an elder so there's a whole pile here. They also request the honor of your presence at a very special Christmas service."

"Are you kidding?" Chet said with undisguised annoyance.

"I'm serious."

"No thanks!"

"They've never had a service like this before," the Sheriff said. "It's in honor of Mr. Terry Alcot."

"Wow!" Terry said. "Why me?"

"The whole town wants to adopt you, Terry. What do you think of that?"

Terry slid his hands into Chet's and Maureen's.

"I'm already adopted," he said.

"That's right," Chet said, clearing his throat. "Just got to get the paperwork."

"This is an honorary adoption," the Sheriff said. He took out a blue-jacketed document. "The Alcots will still be your parents, Terry, but you'll be a Favorite Son. I've got the official resolution right here."

Maureen gave Chet's hand a secret squeeze.

The Sheriff turned to Delmar and Lester.

"Haven't you two birds got something for the Alcots too?" he said.

Delmar and Lester sprang into action and opened the storage compartments of their snowmobiles. They each took out an enormous pie.

"Mildred sent over a mince," Lester said. "Merry

Christmas."

"Wanda sent blueberry," Delmar grinned. "Merry Christmas too."

❄ ❄ ❄

35

The twins scrambled aboard the snowmobiles behind the Deputies while Terry rode in the place of honor with the Sheriff. Chet and Maureen got to ride in the sled where the presents had been.

"Can I steer?" Terry asked.

"All the way there," the Sheriff said.

He flicked on his blue flasher and so did the Deputies. They took off with a roar and soared over the drifts in close formation. The cold air bit at their cheeks as they glided through a fantasy land of white and swept past miles of tall pines whose boughs drooped low under capes of snow. Their rippling bow waves sprayed light powder over windfalls, and flushed quail and jack rabbits out of their burrows.

They rode right up to the church on sidewalks that had not been cleared of snow. The Sheriff gave his siren a quick little blast. When the shriek died down they could hear the choir singing.

Chet quickly drew the Sheriff aside.

"I'd like you to find something out for me," he

said. "An old Indian spent a few days with us this week."

"They show up now and then," the Sheriff said. "Did he steal something?"

"No. He just disappeared."

"They do that too."

"We'd like to make sure he's not—"

"Frozen solid in one of those snow drifts? They do that too."

"The kids took a liking to the old man," Chet said. "We want to be sure he made it home, wherever that is."

"What's his name?" the Sheriff said and took out his notebook. "Getting their names right is the tricky part."

"Okeemakeequid," Chet said.

"Okee-what?"

Chet spelled it out for him while the Sheriff wrote it down. The Sheriff squinted at the name, pronounced it to himself and snapped his notebook closed.

"I'll see what I can find out," he said abruptly. "But you folks better go inside. They're waitin' on you."

The Sheriff and his Deputies ushered them up the stairs. The Sheriff motioned for Terry to get in front, followed by the twins. Then Maureen took Chet by the arm and stood behind the children.

"Ready boys?" Sheriff Hobbs said.

On signal, Delmar and Lester opened the doors.

Inside, the church was aglow with shimmering light. Everybody was holding a lighted candle that flickered from the sudden draft. It was as if a spirit had moved through the church. The entire congregation turned to look at the Alcots and raised up their voices with the choir.

Tears rolled down Maureen's face as Reverend Hipwood made the long walk down the center aisle. He came up to them and took her and Chet by the hand.

"Can you forgive and old fool?" he asked. "I hope so, because this house of fools begs your forgiveness and welcomes you to our humble church—if you'll have us. It's people like you who give Christmas its meaning, and who bring the Spirit of Christmas home to the rest of us."

"Thank you Reverend," Maureen said. "We're very honored."

Reverend Hipwood took Terry by the hand and led him and the twins to the pew that had been reserved for them. Maureen took Chet by the arm and followed. Maureen leaned over to Chet.

"There's so much brotherly love in here I can't stand it," she whispered through a smile. "Sound familiar?"

"I can stand it now," Chet said softly. "At this magical time of year, all kinds of strange things come true."

They joined in the singing that celebrated that special moment on that special day, and their hearts were filled with the joy of Christmas.

❄ ❄ ❄

36

After the church service, Mudge buttonholed Chet.

Say Alcot," he said. "When will I be able to advertise in that Chronicle of yours? I'm overstocked and undersold."

Chet thought about it.

"How about a Day-After-Christmas Sale?" he said.

Mudge's face wrinkled into a frown.

"A sale won't work," he said. "Have to cut the prices. But a special might."

Sheriff Hobbs caught Chet by the sleeve and led him to one side.

"That old Indian you were asking about?" he said. "There's no such person."

"There has to be," Chet said. "He stayed with us."

"I talked to the people at the Chippewa reservation in Mount Pleasant," the Sheriff said. "They never had anybody there by that name."

"Maybe he's not a Chippewa."

"The name is."

Sheriff Hobbs unfolded a piece of paper and put on his glasses.

"Okeemakeequid was the chief who represented the Chippewa at the grand council of Prairie du Chien in Wisconsin," he said, reading from the paper. "The council included chiefs from the Sauk and Fox tribes, the Menominee, the Potawatomi, the Iowa, the Sioux, the Ottawa, the Winnebago and representatives of the U.S. Government. The Treaty was signed in 1825."

"1825!" Chet said. "That would make him over two hundred years old!"

Maureen and the kids came up to them.

"Merry Christmas, Sheriff," she said. "I hope you're going to stop by the house later for some Christmas cheer—and a piece of Mildred's and Wanda's pies."

"Thank you," the Sheriff said, doffing his helmet. "I'll make sure that I do. And Merry Christmas to you—and you, and you, and you," he said to the kids.

"Merry Christmas, Sheriff," the kids said.

"Do I get to ride back with you?" Terry asked.

"You bet you do!" the Sheriff said.

Maureen looked around. "I don't see Sam Slocum."

"That's right," Chet said. "Isn't he here?"

"Sam doesn't do much worshipping in public," the Sheriff said. "In fact Sam doesn't do much worshipping at all since Ella died. He's a very private man. But he sent you this."

The Sheriff took an envelope out of his jacket pocket and passed it to Chet. Chet opened it and looked at it. It was a Christmas card. He read it, smiled and passed it to Maureen.

"Merry Christmas," Maureen said, reading from the card. "See you at the Chronicle with our first big story!"

Before they could say anything Chet and Maureen were slowly engulfed by their new friends, all of whom wanted to wish them a very warm and a very Merry Christmas.